U0025391

Tales from Shakespeare

Macbeth
&
King Lear

悅讀莎士比亞故事(2)

馬。克。白。

李。爾。王。

Charles and Mary Lamb

CONTENTS

CONTENTS

附本

威廉・莎士比亞（William Shakespeare, 1564-1616）

Shakespeare Centre, Henley St, Stratford-upon-Avon, Warwickshire

莎士比亞簡介

陳敬旻

威廉・莎士比亞（William Shakespeare）出生於英國的史特拉福（Stratford-upon-Avon）。莎士比亞的父親曾任地方議員，母親是地主的女兒。莎士比亞對婦女在廚房或起居室裡勞動的描繪不少，這大概是經由觀察母親所得。他本人也懂得園藝，故作品中的植草種樹表現鮮活。

1571 年，莎士比亞進入公立學校就讀，校內教學多採拉丁文，因此在其作品中到處可見到羅馬詩人奧維德（Ovid）的影子。當時代古典文學的英譯日漸普遍，有學者認為莎士比亞只懂得英語，但這種說法有可議之處。舉例來說，在高登的譯本裡，森林女神只用 Diana 這個名字，而莎士比亞卻在《仲夏夜之夢》一劇中用奧維德原作中的 Titania 一名來稱呼仙后。和莎士比亞有私交的文學家班・強生（Ben Jonson）則曾說，莎翁「懂得一點拉丁文，和一點點希臘文」。

莎士比亞的劇本亦常引用聖經典故，顯示他對新舊約也頗為熟悉。在伊麗莎白女王時期，通俗英語中已有很多聖經詞語。此外，莎士比亞應該很知悉當時代年輕人所流行的遊戲娛樂，當時也應該有巡迴劇團不時前來史特拉福演出。 1575 年，伊麗莎白女王來到郡上時，當地人以化裝遊行、假面戲劇、煙火來款待女王，《仲夏夜之夢》裡就有這種盛會的描繪。

1582 年，莎士比亞與安‧海瑟威（Anne Hathaway）結婚，但這場婚姻顯得草率，連莎士比亞的雙親都因不知情而沒有出席婚禮。1586 年，他們在倫敦定居下來。 1586 年的倫敦已是英國首都，年輕人莫不想在此大展抱負。史特拉福與倫敦之間的交通頻仍，但對身無長物的人而言，步行仍是最平常的旅行方式。伊麗莎白時期的文學家喜好步行， 1618 年，班‧強生就曾在倫敦與愛丁堡之間徒步來回。

莎士比亞初抵倫敦的史料不充足，引發諸多揣測。其中一說為莎士比亞曾在律師處當職員，因為他在劇本與詩歌中經常提及法律術語。但這種說法站不住腳，因為莎士比亞多有訛用，例如他在《威尼斯商人》和《一報還一報》中提到的法律原理及程序，就有諸多錯誤。

事實上，伊麗莎白時期的作家都喜歡引用法律詞彙，這是因為當時的文人和律師時有往來，而且中產階級也常介入訴訟案件，許多法律術語自然為常人所知。莎士比亞樂於援用法律術語，這顯示了他對當代生活和風尚的興趣。莎士比亞自抵達倫敦到告老還鄉，心思始終放在戲劇和詩歌上，不太可能接受法律這門專業領域的訓練。

莎士比亞在倫敦的第一份工作是劇場工作。當時常態營業的劇場有兩個：「劇場」（the Theatre）和「帷幕」（the Curtain）。「劇場」的所有人為詹姆士·波比奇（James Burbage），莎士比亞就在此落腳。「劇場」財務狀況不佳，1596 年波比奇過世，把「劇場」交給兩個兒子，其中一個兒子便是著名的悲劇演員理查·波比奇（Richard Burbage）。後來「劇場」因租約問題無法解決，決定將原有的建築物拆除，在泰晤士河的對面重建，改名為「環球」（the Globe）。不久，「環球」就展開了戲劇史上空前繁榮的時代。

伊麗莎白時期的戲劇表演只有男演員，所有的女性角色都由男性擔任。演員反串時會戴上面具，效果十足，然而這並不損故事的意境。莎士比亞本身也是一位出色的演員，曾在《皆大歡喜》和《哈姆雷特》中分別扮演忠僕亞當和國王鬼魂這兩個角色。

莎士比亞很留意演員的說白道詞，這點可從哈姆雷特告誡伶人的對話中窺知一二。莎士比亞熟稔劇場的技術與運作，加上他也是劇場股東，故對劇場的營運和組織都甚有研究。不過，他的志業不在演出或劇場管理，而是劇本和詩歌創作。

莎士比亞的戲劇創作始於 1591 年，他當時真正師法的對象是擅長喜劇的約翰·李利（John Lyly），以及曾寫下轟動一時的悲劇《帖木兒大帝》（*Tamburlaine the Great*）的克里斯多夫·馬婁（Christopher Marlowe）。莎翁戲劇的特色是兼容並蓄，吸收各家長處，而且他也勤奮多產。一直到 1611 年封筆之前，他每年平均寫出兩部劇作和三卷詩作。莎士比亞慣於在既有的文學作品中尋找材料，又重視大眾喜好，常能讓平淡無奇的作品廣受喜愛。

在當時，劇本都是賣斷給劇場，不能再賣給出版商，因此莎劇的出版先後，並不能反映其創作的時間先後。莎翁作品的先後順序都由後人所推斷，推測的主要依據是作品題材和韻格。他早期的戲劇作品，無論悲劇或喜劇，性質都很單純。隨著創作的手法逐漸成熟，內容愈來愈複雜深刻，悲喜劇熔冶一爐。

自 1591 年席德尼爵士（Sir Philip Sidney）的十四行詩集發表後，十四行詩（sonnets，另譯為商籟）在英國即普遍受到文人的喜愛與仿傚。其中許多作品承續佩脫拉克（Petrarch）的風格，多描寫愛情的酸甜苦樂。莎士比亞的創作一向很能反應當時代的文學風尚，在詩歌體裁鼎盛之時，他也將才華展現在十四行詩上，並將部分作品寫入劇本之中。

莎士比亞的十四行詩主要有兩個主題：婚姻責任和詩歌的不朽。這兩者皆是文藝復興時期詩歌中常見的主題。不少人以為莎士比亞的十四行詩表達了他個人的自省與懺悔，但事實上這些內容有更多是源於他的戲劇天分。

1595 年至 1598 年，莎士比亞陸續寫了《羅密歐與茱麗葉》、《仲夏夜之夢》、《馴悍記》、《威尼斯商人》和若干歷史劇，他的詩歌戲劇也在這段時期受到肯定。當時代的梅爾斯（Francis Meres）就將莎士比亞視為最偉大的文學家，他說：「要是繆思會說英語，一定也會喜歡引用莎士比亞的精彩語藻。」「無論是悲劇或喜劇，莎士比亞的表現都是首屈一指。」

闊別故鄉十一年後，莎士比亞於 1596 年返回故居，並在隔年買下名為「新居」（New Place）的房子。那是鎮上第二大的房子，他大幅改建整修，爾後家道日益興盛。莎士比亞有足夠的財力置產並不足以為奇，但他大筆的固定收入主要來自表演，而非劇本創作。當時不乏有成功的演員靠演戲發財，甚至有人將這種現象寫成劇本。

除了表演之外，劇場行政及管理的工作，還有宮廷演出的賞賜，都是他的財源。許多文獻均顯示，莎士比亞是個非常關心財富、地產和社會地位的人，讓許多人感到與他的詩人形象有些扞格不入。

伊麗莎白女王過世後，詹姆士一世（James I）於 1603 年登基，他把莎士比亞所屬的劇團納入保護。莎士比亞此時寫了《第十二夜》和佳評如潮的《哈姆雷特》，成就傲視全英格蘭。但他仍謙恭有禮、溫文爾雅，一如十多前年初抵倫敦的樣子，因此也愈發受到大眾的喜愛。

從這一年起，莎士比亞開始撰寫悲劇《奧賽羅》。他寫悲劇並非是因為精神壓力或生活變故，而是身為一名劇作家，最終目的就是要寫出優秀的悲劇作品。當時他嘗試以詩入劇，在《哈姆雷特》和《一報還一報》中尤其爐火純青。隨後《李爾王》和《馬克白》問世，一直到四年後的《安東尼與克麗奧佩脫拉》，寫作風格登峰造極。

1609 年，倫敦瘟疫猖獗，隔年不見好轉，46 歲的莎士比亞決定告別倫敦，返回史特拉福退隱。 1616 年，莎士比亞和老友德雷頓、班‧強生聚會時，可能由於喝得過於盡興，回家後發高燒，一病不起。他將遺囑修改完畢，同年 4 月 23 日，恰巧在他 52 歲的生日當天去世。

七年後，昔日的劇團好友收錄他的劇本做為全集出版，其中有喜劇、歷史劇、悲劇等共 36 個劇本。此書不僅不負莎翁本人所託，也為後人留下珍貴而豐富的文化資源，其中不僅包括美妙動人的詞句，還有各種人物的性格塑造，如高貴、低微、嚴肅或歡樂等性格的著墨。

除了作品，莎士比亞本人也在生前受到讚揚。班·強生曾說他是個「正人君子，天性開放自由，想像力出奇，擁有大無畏的思想，言詞溫和，蘊含機智。」也有學者以勇敢、敏感、平衡、幽默和身心健康這五種特質來形容莎士比亞，並說他「將無私的愛奉為至上，認為罪惡的根源是恐懼，而非金錢。」

值得一提的是，有人認為這些劇本刻畫入微，具有知性，不可能是未受過大學教育的莎士比亞所寫，因而引發爭議。有人就此推測真正的作者，其中較為人知的有法蘭西斯·培根（Francis Bacon）和牛津的德維爾公爵（Edward de Vere of Oxford），後者形成了頗具影響力的牛津學派。儘管傳說繪聲繪影，各種假說和研究不斷，但大概已經沒有人會懷疑確有莎士比亞這個人的存在了。

作者簡介：蘭姆姐弟

姐姐瑪麗（Mary Lamb）生於 1764 年，弟弟查爾斯（Charles Lamb）於 1775 年也在倫敦呱呱落地。因為家境不夠寬裕，瑪麗沒有接受過完整的教育。她從小就做針線活，幫忙持家，照顧母親。查爾斯在學生時代結識了詩人柯立芝（Samuel Taylor Coleridge），兩人成為終生的朋友。查爾斯後來因家中經濟困難而輟學， 1792 年轉而就職於東印度公司（East India House），這是他謀生的終身職業。

查爾斯在二十歲時一度精神崩潰，瑪麗則因為長年工作過量，在 1796 年突然精神病發，持刀攻擊父母，母親不幸傷重身亡。這件人倫悲劇發生後，瑪麗被判為精神異常，送往精神病院。查爾斯為此放棄自己原本期待的婚姻，以便全心照顧姐姐，使她免於在精神病院終老。

十九世紀的英國教育重視莎翁作品，一般的中產階級家庭也希望孩子早點接觸莎劇。1806 年，文學家兼編輯高德溫（William Godwin）邀請查爾斯協助「少年圖書館」的出版計畫，請他將莎翁的劇本改寫為適合兒童閱讀的故事。

查爾斯接受這項工作後就與瑪麗合作，他負責六齣悲劇，瑪麗負責十四齣喜劇並撰寫前言。瑪麗在後來曾描述說，他們兩人「就坐在同一張桌子上改寫，看起來就好像《仲夏夜之夢》裡的荷米雅與海蓮娜一樣。」就這樣，姐弟兩人合力完成了這一系列的莎士比亞故事。《莎士比亞故事集》在 1807 年出版後便大受好評，建立了查爾斯的文學聲譽。

查爾斯的寫作風格獨特，筆法樸實，主題豐富。他將自己的一生，包括童年時代、基督教會學校的生活、東印度公司的光陰、與瑪麗相伴的點點滴滴，以及自己的白日夢、鍾愛的書籍和友人等等，都融入在文章裡，作品充滿細膩情感和豐富的想像力。他的軟弱、怪異、魅力、幽默、口吃，在在都使讀者感到親切熟悉，而獨特的筆法與敘事方式，也使他成為英國出色的散文大師。

1823 年，查爾斯和瑪麗領養了一個孤兒愛瑪。兩年後，查爾斯自東印度公司退休，獲得豐厚的退休金。查爾斯的健康情形和瑪麗的精神狀況卻每況愈下。 1833 年，愛瑪嫁給出版商後，又只剩下姐弟兩人。 1834 年 7 月，由於幼年時代的好友柯立芝去世，查爾斯的精神一蹶不振，沉湎酒精。此年秋天，查爾斯在散步時不慎跌倒，傷及顏面，後來傷口竟惡化至不可收拾的地步，而於年底過世。

查爾斯善與人交，他和同時期的許多文人都保持良好情誼，又因他一生對姐姐的照顧不餘遺力，所以也廣受敬佩。查爾斯和瑪麗兩人都終生未婚，查爾斯曾在一篇伊利亞小品中，將他們的狀況形容為「雙重單身」（double singleness）。查爾斯去世後，瑪麗的心理狀態雖然漸趨惡化，但仍繼續活了十三年之久。

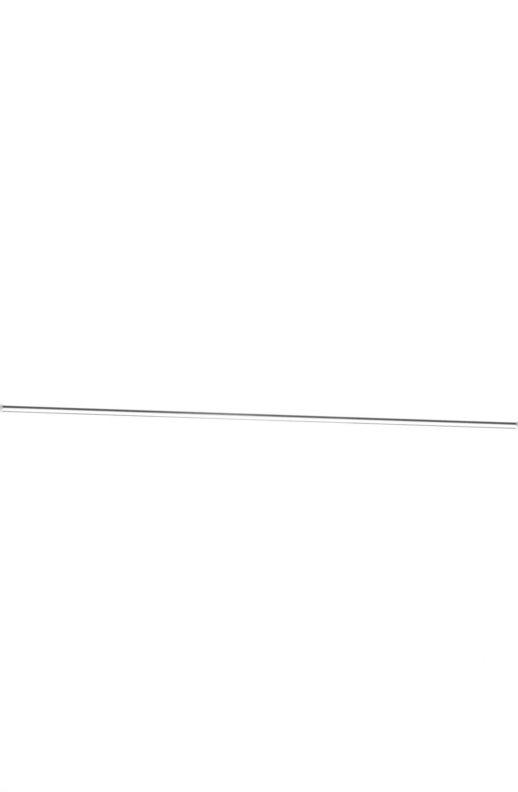

Macbeth

馬克白

導讀

弒君之滔天大罪

1603 年，莎士比亞所屬的劇團正式成為英格蘭國王詹姆士一世的國王御前劇團（King's Men），劇中的團員莫不對國王充滿感謝與敬意，並盡可能迎合國王的興趣喜好以表達效忠之意，其中最明顯的例子，就是莎士比亞於 1606 年寫成時就備受爭議的《馬克白》。

這個故事源自於何林塞（Raphael Holinshed）在 1587 年出版的《英格蘭、蘇格蘭及愛爾蘭編年史》（*Chronicles of England, Scotland, and Ireland*）。史實是馬克白和班科聯手殺害年輕羸弱的鄧肯國王，之後馬克白風光榮耀地在位十年，但莎士比亞改編成馬克白夫婦謀殺鄧肯國王，把詹姆士一世的祖先班科排除於謀殺之外。

詹姆士一世的雙親遇害身亡，使得他對暗殺特別感到恐懼。他篤信君權神授之說，認為弒君是萬惡不赦的罪行，不僅有害於個人與國家，同時也會破壞宇宙的秩序。詹姆士對巫術極有研究，曾經在 1599 年出版過《魔鬼學》（*Demonology*），他相信巫術，也認定有巫婆曾共謀要加害於他，他因此舉行許多儀式，降魔除邪，並進而鞏固王權。

馬克白對弒君的恐懼也反映了王權的至上。他知道自己所要犯下的是滔天大罪，因此不斷受到良心的折磨。鄧肯特別恩寵馬克白，馬克白沒有理由謀殺他，然而；當馬克白做了謀殺的決定之後，整齣戲便充滿神秘邪惡的氣氛。馬克白利慾薰心，但野心會受到道德和宗教的規範，馬克白反覆思考，基於自己、鄧肯、人民、正義等因素，他也認為自己應該打消弒君的念頭，但為什麼還是下了毒手呢？

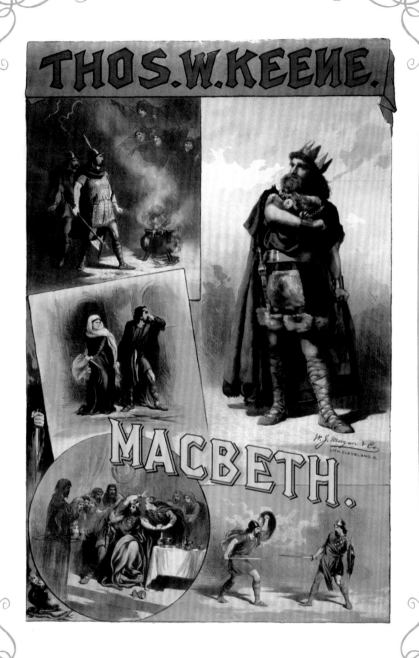

利慾薰心的馬克白夫人

促使他改變心意的是馬克白夫
人。馬克白夫人一出場就正在看
馬克白捎來的信，馬克白夫人不
同於一般女性，她極力慫恿馬克
白弒君。武將出身的馬克白重視
榮耀與勝利，最不能忍受被批評
膽小懦弱。他有擁有權勢的深層
慾望，想證明自己的男子氣概，
馬克白夫人掌握住他的這種性
格，用激將法來防止他落入恐懼
和罪惡感之中。

LADY MACBETH

在十六世紀享有惡名的馬基爾維
利（Niccolo Machiavelli）曾在《君王論》（*Discourses*）裡提到：「人
不用再為需求而戰時，就會為權力而戰。無論擁有了何等地位，這
種強烈情緒都揮之不去。」而且「人對無法獲得的東西特別渴望」，
如果殺害鄧肯能夠洗去懦弱之名，又能一夕之間登上王位，滿足自
己與夫人的野心和權力慾望，何不放手一搏呢？更何況他還有女巫
的預言，像是有了無形的靠山和保證一樣。如馬基爾維利所言，渴
望一逞其慾的馬克白不擇手段，終於鑄下了無可挽回的錯誤。

三位命運女神

劇中人物稱那三個長了鬍鬚的怪婦人為女巫，但劇中人物表上稱她們為三女神（Weird Sisters，原來的拼法是 weyrd 或 weyward，而 weyward 又與「任性剛愎」、「難以管束」的 wayward 同音）。weird 一字在古英文裡有「命運」之意，何林塞的《編年史》裡就將三個詭異姊妹比喻為「命運的女神」，主宰人類命運，但這三位命運女神並不是促使馬克白下手的主要因素。

伊莉莎白時期的人們認為，女巫是魔鬼的僕從，她們不會不請自來，而是受到潛意識或下意識的邪念所召喚而來，況且女巫也沒有左右或強迫他人的能力，只能以幻化的未來影像來引誘他人做某些事。亦即，正因馬克白有造反念頭在先，才會引發女巫來訪。

在《馬克白》一劇中，語言常常模稜兩可，具有雙重含義，造成誤導誤解。這種語言既不能代表真實，但也非子虛烏有。女巫的話讓馬克白興致勃勃，直到事實發生後，才知不過是一場謊言空夢。然而一直到劇末，女巫都不像馬克白夫婦一樣遭受懲罰報應。在莎士比亞時代，獵巫行動還時有所聞，但是此劇對女巫的後果完全沒有交代，只是將他們短暫的懸置在觀眾的心中。

人性與道德的深刻描繪

莎劇評論家卜瑞黎（A. C. Bradley）指出，《馬》劇讓人聯想到的，幾乎都是夜晚或黑暗角落的場景。此劇表現的正是人類與黑暗交手之後的結果──邪惡戰勝人性和文明。馬克白清楚是非道德，明白邪惡的誘惑，卻仍擇惡去善，象徵出人性的墮落。但此劇決非傳統上勸人離惡向善的「道德劇」（morality play），因為它不以馬克白最終遭到報應為快，而是在於描繪邪惡面的心理效應。

MACBETH

馬克白心中早已蟄伏野心，問題的關鍵是這種野心如何被引發。莎士比亞極少將焦點集中在主要角色的罪惡上，但馬克白赤裸裸的人性，卻能使觀眾了解、同情，甚至認同該角色。我們目睹馬克白一連串過程中的掙扎、夢魘、不安，以及不可避免的一錯再錯。他知道邪惡的後果，但他又不可自拔。與其將馬克白的墮落歸咎於命運，不如說是性格所造成的。相較於馬克白，馬克白夫人對罪惡就顯得麻木不仁。她為人冷靜，思慮周密，唆使馬克白犯下滔天罪行，但當馬克白為幻象所苦時，她並沒有被良心所折磨。

戲劇的特色

第一對開本裡將本劇歸為悲劇而非歷史劇，或許是因為劇中都是蘇格蘭人，而非英格蘭人。但這個劇本在許多詩人及文學評論家的眼中，都遠比歷史劇精彩。劇中有巫術、謀殺、復辟，也摻有歷史根據和犯罪心理學，馬克白的許多獨白也充滿雋永詩意。

馬克白的性情和情緒，如威風、懷疑、恐懼、憤怒、絕望、決心和過度壓抑等等，都是《馬》劇長久以來吸引無數觀眾及讀者的重要原因。馬克白夫人則是莎翁悲劇中最具挑戰性的女性角色，著名的女演員如席登絲（Sarah Siddons）、湯芮（Ellen Terry）、鄧琪（Judi Dench）等都曾有過出色的詮釋。

本劇在十九世紀的演出多注重寫實的場景，到了二十世紀，舞台普遍傾向簡單空白，表現出心理禁閉的張力。

與莎翁其他悲劇相較之下，《馬克白》的劇本篇幅簡短很多，因此有人推測，在 1606 年首演至 1623 年莎士比亞全集第一對開本（the First Folio）首度問世之間，曾有人刪改過劇本。雖然劇中有若干前後矛盾之處，但是並沒有足夠證據可以證明此劇的確經過刪減，或經何人刪減。而且就算真有刪減一事，也無傷《馬》劇的精神。

LADY MACBETH

另一方面，也有部分批評家認為此劇被添加了內容，這種說法則有較為令人信服的證據。本劇中有兩景顯得特別突兀，例如女巫之王黑可娣（Hecate）的出現唐突，景內的韻文和劇本其他各處不合，內容類似彌德頓（Thomas Middleton）的《巫婆》（*The Witch*）。因此一般相信增寫人就是彌德頓，蘭姆改寫的這個版本，就略去了黑可娣這個角色。

人物表

Macbeth	馬克白	故事的男主人翁，將軍出身，弒君奪位
Lady Macbeth	馬克白夫人	故事的女主人翁，慫恿丈夫弒君奪位
Three Weird Sisters	三女巫	住在荒野中的預言者
Duncan	鄧肯國王	一位仁君，遭馬克白刺殺
Malcolm	梅爾康	鄧肯國王之長子
Donalbain	杜納班	鄧肯國王之么子
Banquo	班科	一位忠心的將軍
Fleance	弗林斯	班科之子
Macduff	麥德夫	一位領主，擁護梅爾康

Macbeth

🎧 **1** When Duncan the Meek[1] reigned King of Scotland, there lived a great thane[2], or lord, called Macbeth. This Macbeth was a near kinsman[3] to the king, and in great esteem at court for his valor and conduct in the wars; an example of which he had lately given, in defeating a rebel army assisted by the troops of Norway in terrible numbers.

The two Scottish generals, Macbeth and Banquo, returning victorious from this great battle, their way lay over a blasted[4] heath[5], where they were stopped by the strange appearance of three figures like women, except that they had beards, and their withered[6] skins and wild attire[7] made them look not like any earthly creatures. Macbeth first addressed them, when they, seemingly offended, laid each one her choppy[8] finger upon her skinny lips, in token of silence; and the first of them saluted Macbeth with the title of Thane of Glamis.

1 meek [miːk] (a.) 溫和的
2 thane [θeɪn] (n.) 藉服兵役而取得土地的大鄉紳
3 kinsman ['kɪnzmən] (n.) 男親戚
4 blasted ['blæstɪd] (a.) 〔文學用法〕被閃電擊毀的
5 heath [hiːθ] (n.) 荒地
6 withered ['wɪðərd] (a.) 乾皺的
7 attire [ə'taɪr] (n.) 〔文學用法〕〔詩的用法〕服裝
8 choppy ['tʃɑːpi] (a.) 多裂縫的

MACBETH

The general was not a little startled to find himself known by such creatures; but how much more, when the second of them followed up that salute by giving him the title of Thane of Cawdor, to which honor he had no pretensions[9]; and again the third bid him "All hail[10]! king that shalt be hereafter!" Such a prophetic greeting might well amaze him, who knew that while the king's sons lived he could not hope to succeed to the throne.

9 pretension [prɪˈtenʃən] (n.) 主張（常用複數形）
10 hail [heɪl] (v.) 歡呼；打招呼

3 Then turning to Banquo, they pronounced him, in a sort of riddling terms, to be *lesser than Macbeth and greater! Not so happy, but much happier!* and prophesied that though he should never reign, yet his sons after him should be kings in Scotland. They then turned into air, and vanished: by which the generals knew them to be the weird sisters, or witches.

While they stood pondering on the strangeness of this adventure, there arrived certain messengers from the king, who were empowered by him to confer upon Macbeth the dignity of Thane of Cawdor.

Banquo.   Look how our partner's rapt.   Act 1. Scene 3.

An event so miraculously corresponding with the prediction of the witches astonished Macbeth, and he stood wrapped in amazement, unable to make reply to the messengers; and in that point of time swelling hopes arose in his mind that the prediction of the third witch might in like manner have its accomplishment, and that he should one day reign king in Scotland.

Turning to Banquo, he said, "Do you not hope that your children shall be kings, when what the witches promised to me has so wonderfully come to pass?"

"That hope," answered the general, "might enkindle[11] you to aim at the throne; but oftentimes these ministers of darkness tell us truths in little things, to betray us into deeds of greatest consequence."

But the wicked suggestions of the witches had sunk too deep into the mind of Macbeth to allow him to attend to the warnings of the good Banquo. From that time he bent all his thoughts on how to compass[12] the throne of Scotland.

Macbeth had a wife, to whom he communicated the strange prediction of the weird sisters, and its partial accomplishment. She was a bad, ambitious woman, and so as her husband and herself could arrive at greatness, she cared not much by what means.

11 enkindle [ɪnˈkɪndl] (v.) 煽動
12 compass [ˈkʌmpəs] (v.) 達到；獲得

She spurred[13] on the reluctant purpose of Macbeth, who felt compunction[14] at the thoughts of blood, and did not cease to represent the murder of the king as a step absolutely necessary to the fulfilment of the flattering prophecy.

Lady Macbeth spurred on the reluctant purpose of Macbeth.

It happened at this time that the king, who out of his royal condescension[15] would oftentimes visit his principal nobility upon gracious terms[16], came to Macbeth's house, attended by his two sons, Malcolm and Donalbain, and a numerous train[17] of thanes and attendants, the more to honor Macbeth for the triumphal success of his wars.

---

13 spur [spɜːr] (v.) 踢馬刺；刺激；激勵
14 compunction [kəmˈpʌŋkʃən] (n.) 良心的不安；內疚
15 condescension [ˌkɑːndɪˈsenʃən] (n.) 屈尊俯就
16 terms [tɜːrmz] (n.) 關係；友誼（作複數形）
17 train [treɪn] (n.) 成縱隊行進的若干人

The castle of Macbeth was pleasantly situated, and the air about it was sweet and wholesome, which appeared by the nests which the martlet, or swallow, had built under all the jutting[18] friezes[19] and buttresses[20] of the building, wherever it found a place of advantage; for where those birds most breed and haunt, the air is observed to be delicate.

The king entered well pleased with the place, and not less so with the attentions and respect of his honored hostess, Lady Macbeth, who had the art of covering treacherous[21] purposes with smiles; and could look like the innocent flower, while she was indeed the serpent[22] under it.

Lady Macbeth. Look like the innocent flower, but be the serpent under it.
Act 1. Scene 5.

18 jutting ['dʒʌtɪŋ] (a.) 伸出的；突出的
19 frieze [friːz] (n.) 壁緣（建築物外部的牆上端之橫幅雕飾帶）
20 buttress ['bʌtrəs] (n.) 拱壁
21 treacherous ['tretʃərəs] (a.) 虛偽的；奸詐的
22 serpent ['sɜːrpənt] (n.)〔譬喻用法〕狡獪之人；心如蛇蠍的人

The king being tired with his journey, went early to bed, and in his stateroom two grooms of his chamber (as was the custom) slept beside him. He had been unusually pleased with his reception, and had made presents before he retired to his principal officers; and among the rest, had sent a rich diamond to Lady Macbeth, greeting her by the name of his most kind hostess.

Now was the middle of night, when over half the world nature seems dead, and wicked dreams abuse men's minds asleep, and none but the wolf and the murderer is abroad. This was the time when Lady Macbeth waked to plot the murder of the king.

She would not have undertaken a deed so abhorrent[23] to her sex, but that she feared her husband's nature, that it was too full of the milk of human kindness[24], to do a contrived[25] murder. She knew him to be ambitious, but withal[26] to be scrupulous[27], and not yet prepared for that height of crime which commonly in the end accompanies inordinate ambition.

23 abhorrent [əbˈɔːrənt] (a.) 可恨的；可惡的
24 the milk of human kindness 人類本性的仁慈；人性的惻隱之心
25 contrive [kənˈtraɪv] (v.) 設計；想辦法；設法完成
26 withal [wɪˈðɔːl] (adv.)〔古代用法〕且；此外
27 scrupulous [ˈskruːpjʊləs] (a.) 多顧慮的

LADY MACBETH

She had won him to consent to the murder, but she doubted his resolution; and she feared that the natural tenderness of his disposition (more humane than her own) would come between, and defeat the purpose.

So with her own hands armed with a dagger, she approached the king's bed; having taken care to ply[28] the grooms of his chamber so with wine, that they slept intoxicated[29], and careless of their charge. There lay Duncan in a sound sleep after the fatigues of his journey, and as she viewed him earnestly, there was something in his face, as he slept, which resembled her own father; and she had not the courage to proceed.

28 ply [plaɪ] (v.) 以……供給某人
29 intoxicated [ɪnˈtɑːksəˌkeɪtɪd] (a.) 喝醉的

🎧10 She returned to confer with her husband. His resolution had begun to stagger[30]. He considered that there were strong reasons against the deed. In the first place, he was not only a subject[31], but a near kinsman to the king; and he had been his host and entertainer that day, whose duty, by the laws of hospitality, it was to shut the door against his murderers, not bear the knife himself.

Then he considered how just and merciful a king this Duncan had been, how clear of offense to his subjects, how loving to his nobility, and in particular to him; that such kings are the peculiar care of heaven, and their subjects doubly bound to revenge their deaths. Besides, by the favors of the king, Macbeth stood high in the opinion of all sorts of men, and how would those honors be stained[32] by the reputation of so foul[33] a murder!

---

30 stagger ['stægər] (v.) 搖搖晃晃;蹣跚而行
31 subject ['sʌbdʒɪkt] (n.) 臣民
32 stain [steɪn] (v.) 污染;玷污
33 foul [faʊl] (a.) 邪惡的;惡劣的

In these conflicts of the mind Lady Macbeth found her husband inclining to the better part, and resolving to proceed no further. But she being a woman not easily shaken from her evil purpose, began to pour in at his ears words which infused a portion of her own spirit into his mind, assigning[34] reason upon reason why he should not shrink from what he had undertaken; how easy the deed was; how soon it would be over; and how the action of one short night would give to all their nights and days to come sovereign[35] sway[36] and royalty!

Then she threw contempt[37] on his change of purpose, and accused him of fickleness[38] and cowardice; and declared that she had given suck, and knew how tender it was to love the babe that milked her; but she would, while it was smiling in her face, have plucked it from her breast, and dashed[39] its brains out, if she had so sworn to do it, as he had sworn to perform that murder.

34 assign [ə'saɪn] (v.) 提出理由
35 sovereign ['sɑːvrən] (a.) 最高統治者的；至高無上的
36 sway [sweɪ] (v.) (n.) 統治；支配
37 contempt [kən'tempt] (n.) 輕視；蔑視
38 fickleness ['fɪkəlnəs] (n.)（指天氣、心情）多變的
39 dash [dæʃ] (v.) 猛擊；猛擲

Act 1, Scene 7

<u>Macbeth</u>

And pity, like a naked newborn babe,
Striding the blast, or heaven's cherubim, horsed
Upon the sightless couriers of the air,
Shall blow the horrid deed in every eye,
That tears shall drown the wind.

PITY (WILLIAM BLAKE, 1795)

Macbeth.　　　Look on it again I dare not.
Lady Macbeth.　Infirm of purpose! Give me the daggers.

Act 2. Scene 2.

Then she added, how practicable it was to lay the guilt of the deed upon the drunken sleepy grooms. And with the valor of her tongue she so chastised[40] his sluggish[41] resolutions, that he once more summoned up courage to the bloody business.

So, taking the dagger in his hand, he softly stole in the dark to the room where Duncan lay; and as he went, he thought he saw another dagger in the air, with the handle toward him, and on the blade and at the point of it drops of blood; but when be tried to grasp at it, it was nothing but air, a mere phantasm[42] proceeding from his own hot and oppressed brain and the business he had in hand.

40 chastise [tʃæˈstaɪz] (v.) 嚴懲；責罰
41 sluggish [ˈslʌgɪʃ] (a.) 懶散的
42 phantasm [ˈfæntæzəm] (n.) 幻影；幻像

Getting rid of this fear, he entered the king's room, whom he despatched[43] with one stroke of his dagger. Just as he had done the murder, one of the grooms, who slept in the chamber, laughed in his sleep, and the other cried, "Murder," which woke them both; but they said a short prayer; one of them said, "God bless us!" and the other answered "Amen;" and addressed themselves to sleep again.

Macbeth, who stood listening to them, tried to say "Amen," when the fellow said, "God bless us!" but, though he had most need of a blessing the word stuck in his throat, and he could not pronounce it.

43 despatch [dɪ'spætʃ] (v.) 殺死；處死

Again he thought he heard a voice which cried, "Sleep no more: Macbeth doth murder sleep, the innocent sleep, that nourishes life." Still it cried, "Sleep no more," to all the house. "Glamis hath murdered sleep, and therefore Cawdor shall sleep no more, Macbeth shall sleep no more."

With such horrible imaginations Macbeth returned to his listening wife, who began to think he had failed of his purpose, and that the deed was somehow frustrated. He came in so distracted[44] a state, that she reproached[45] him with his want of firmness, and sent him to wash his hands of the blood which stained them, while she took his dagger, with purpose to stain the cheeks of the grooms with blood, to make it seem their guilt.

---

44 distracted [dɪ'stræktɪd] (a.) 心情紛亂的；困擾的
45 reproach [rɪ'proʊtʃ] (v.) 責備

🎧15 Morning came, and with it the discovery of the murder, which could not be concealed; and though Macbeth and his lady made great show of grief, and the proofs against the grooms (the dagger being produced against them and their faces smeared[46] with blood) were sufficiently strong, yet the entire suspicion fell upon Macbeth, whose inducements[47] to such a deed were so much more forcible than such poor silly grooms could be supposed to have; and Duncan's two sons fled. Malcolm, the eldest, sought for refuge in the English court; and the youngest, Donalbain, made his escape to Ireland.

The king's sons, who should have succeeded him, having thus vacated[48] the throne, Macbeth as next heir was crowned king, and thus the prediction of the weird sisters was literally accomplished.

---

46 smear [smɪr] (v.) 塗抹;弄髒
47 inducement [ɪnˈduːsmənt] (n.) 誘因;動機
48 vacate [ˈveɪkeɪt] (v.)〔正式用法〕放棄

LADY MACBETH

🎧16 Though placed so high, Macbeth and his queen could not forget the prophecy of the weird sisters, that, though Macbeth should be king, yet not his children, but the children of Banquo, should be kings after him. The thought of this, and that they had defiled[49] their hands with blood, and done so great crimes, only to place the posterity[50] of Banquo upon the throne, so rankled[51] within them, that they determined to put to death both Banquo and his son, to make void the predictions of the weird sisters, which in their own case had been so remarkably brought to pass.

For this purpose they made a great supper, to which they invited all the chief thanes; and, among the rest, with marks of particular respect, Banquo and his son Fleance were invited.

49 defile [dɪˈfaɪl] (v.) 弄髒；玷污
50 posterity [pɑːˈsterɪti] (n.) 子孫後代
51 rankle [ˈræŋkəl] (v.) 使人痛心

🎧(17) The way by which Banquo was to pass to the palace at night was beset[52] by murderers appointed by Macbeth, who stabbed Banquo; but in the scuffle[53] Fleance escaped.

From that Fleance descended a race of monarchs[54] who afterwards filled the Scottish throne, ending with James the Sixth of Scotland and the First of England, under whom the two crowns of England and Scotland were united.

52 beset [bɪ'sɛt] (v.) 包圍；圍困
53 scuffle ['skʌfəl] (n.) 混戰
54 monarch ['mɑːnərk] (n.) 君主；最高統治者

🎧 (18) At supper, the queen, whose manners were in the highest degree affable[55] and royal, played the hostess with a gracefulness and attention which conciliated[56] everyone present, and Macbeth discoursed freely with his thanes and nobles, saying, that all that was honorable in the country was under his roof, if he had but his good friend Banquo present, whom yet he hoped he should rather have to chide for neglect, than to lament for any mischance[57].

Just at these words the ghost of Banquo, whom he had caused to be murdered, entered the room and placed himself on the chair which Macbeth was about to occupy. Though Macbeth was a bold man, and one that could have faced the devil without trembling, at this horrible sight his cheeks turned white with fear, and he stood quite unmanned[58] with his eyes fixed upon the ghost.

55 affable [ˈæfəbəl] (a.) 和善有禮的；和藹可親的
56 conciliate [kənˈsɪlieɪt] (v.) 贏得支持或友情
57 mischance [mɪsˈtʃæns] (n.) 不幸
58 unmanned [ʌnˈmænd] (a.) 缺乏人員的

🎧 19 His queen and all the nobles, who saw nothing, but perceived him gazing (as they thought) upon an empty chair, took it for a fit of distraction; and she reproached him, whispering that it was but the same fancy which made him see the dagger in the air, when he was about to kill Duncan. But Macbeth continued to see the ghost, and gave no heed to all they could say, while he addressed it with distracted words, yet so significant, that his queen, fearing the dreadful secret would be disclosed, in great haste dismissed the guests, excusing the infirmity of Macbeth as a disorder he was often troubled with.

Macbeth.   Which of you have done this?
Lords.   What, my good lord?
Macbeth.   Thou canst not say I did it.   Act 3. Scene 4.

🎧 20 To such dreadful fancies Macbeth was subject[59]. His queen and he had their sleeps afflicted[60] with terrible dreams, and the blood of Banquo troubled them not more than the escape of Fleance, whom now they looked upon as father to a line of kings who should keep their posterity out of the throne. With these miserable thoughts they found no peace, and Macbeth determined once more to seek out the weird sisters, and know from them the worst.

He sought them in a cave upon the heath, where they, who knew by foresight of his coming, were engaged in preparing their dreadful charms, by which they conjured[61] up infernal[62] spirits to reveal to them futurity.

Macbeth. How now, you secret, black, and midnight hags?
          What is't you do?
All.   A deed without a name.   Act 4. Scene 1.

59 subject ['sʌbdʒɪkt] (a.) 受支配的
60 afflict [ə'flɪkt] (v.) 使痛苦；折磨
61 conjure ['kʌndʒər] (v.) 使從虛無中顯現
62 infernal [ɪn'fɜːrnl] (a.) 地獄的；惡魔般的；可憎的

🎧(21) Their horrid ingredients were toads, bats, and serpents, the eye of a newt[63], and the tongue of a dog, the leg of a lizard, and the wing of the night-owl, the scale of a dragon, the tooth of a wolf, the maw of the ravenous salt-sea shark, the mummy of a witch, the root of the poisonous hemlock[64] (this to have effect must be digged in the dark), the gall of a goat, and the liver of a Jew, with slips[65] of the yew[66] tree that roots itself in graves, and the finger of a dead child.

All these were set on to boil in a great kettle, or caldron, which, as fast as it grew too hot, was cooled with a baboon's[67] blood: to these they poured in the blood of a sow[68] that had eaten her young, and they threw into the flame the grease that had sweaten from a murderer's gibbet[69]. By these charms they bound the infernal spirits to answer their questions.

63 newt [nuːt] (n.) 蠑螈；水蜥
64 hemlock ['hemlɑːk] (n.) 毒芹（歐洲一種很常見的有毒香草）
65 slip [slɪp] (n.)（種植用的）接枝
66 yew [juː] (n.) 紫杉；水松
67 baboon [bæ'buːn] (n.) 狒狒
68 sow [soʊ] (n.) 母豬
69 gibbet ['dʒɪbɪt] (n.) 絞架；絞刑臺

(22) It was demanded of Macbeth, whether he would have his doubts resolved by them, or by their masters, the spirits. He, nothing daunted[70] by the dreadful ceremonies which be saw, boldly answered, "Where are they? let me see them." And they called the spirits, which were three.

And the first arose in the likeness of an armed head, and he called Macbeth by name, and bid him beware of the Thane of Fife; for which caution Macbeth thanked him; for Macbeth had entertained[71] a jealousy of Macduff, the Thane of Fife.

And the second spirit arose in the likeness of a bloody child, and he called Macbeth by name, and bid him have no fear, but laugh to scorn[72] the power of man, for none of woman born should have power to hurt him; and he advised him to be bloody, bold, and resolute.

"Then live, Macduff" cried the king; "what need I fear of thee? but yet I will make assurance doubly sure. Thou shalt not live; that I may tell pale-hearted fear it lies, and sleep in spite of thunder."

---

70 daunt [dɑːnt] (v.) 挫折；使氣餒
71 entertain [ˌentərˈteɪn] (v.) 心懷
72 scorn [skɔːrn] (v.) 輕蔑；藐視

(23) That spirit being
dismissed, a third arose
in the form of a child
crowned, with a tree
in his hand. He called
Macbeth by name, and
comforted him against
conspiracies[73], saying,
that he should never
be vanquished[74], until
the wood of Birnam to
Dunsinane Hill should
come against him.

"Sweet bodements[75]! good!" cried Macbeth; "who
can unfix the forest, and move it from its earthbound
roots? I see I shall live the usual period of man's life,
and not be cut off by a violent death. But my heart
throbs[76] to know one thing. Tell me, if your art can
tell so much, if Banquo's issue shall ever reign in this
kingdom?"

73 conspiracy [kən'spɪrəsi] (n.) 陰謀;共謀
74 vanquish ['væŋkwɪʃ] (v.) 征服;擊敗
75 bodement ['boʊdmənt] (n.) 〔舊式用法〕〔詩的用法〕預兆
76 throb [θrɑːb] (v.) 跳動;悸動

🎧 24   Here the caldron sank into the ground, and a noise of music was heard, and eight shadows, like kings, passed by Macbeth, and Banquo last, who bore a glass which showed the figures of many more, and Banquo all bloody smiled upon Macbeth, and pointed to them; by which Macbeth knew that these were the posterity of Banquo, who should reign after him in Scotland; and the witches, with a sound of soft music, and with dancing, making a show of duty and welcome to Macbeth, vanished. And from this time the thoughts of Macbeth were all bloody and dreadful.

The first thing he heard when he got out of the witches' cave, was that Macduff, Thane of Fife, had fled[77] to England, to join the army which was forming against him under Malcolm, the eldest son of the late king, with intent to displace Macbeth, and set Malcolm, the rightful heir, upon the throne.

77 flee [fliː] (v.) 逃

Son of Macduff.　He has kill'd me, mother.
　　　　　　　　Run away, I pray you.　　　Act 4. Scene 2.

(25)　Macbeth, stung with rage, set upon the castle of Macduff, and put his wife and children, whom the thane had left behind, to the sword, and extended the slaughter[78] to all who claimed the least relationship to Macduff.

---

78 slaughter ['slɔːtə] (n.) 殺戮；屠殺

🎧26 These and suchlike deeds alienated[79] the minds of all his chief nobility from him. Such as could, fled to join with Malcolm and Macduff, who were now approaching with a powerful army, which they had raised in England; and the rest secretly wished success to their arms, though for fear of Macbeth they could take no active part. His recruits[80] went on slowly.

Everybody hated the tyrant; nobody loved or honored him; but all suspected him, and he began to envy the condition of Duncan, whom he had murdered, who slept soundly in his grave, against whom treason[81] had done its worst: steel nor poison, domestic malice[82] nor foreign levies[83], could hurt him any longer.

---

79 alienate ['eɪlɪəneɪt] (v.) 使疏遠；使不和
80 recruit [rɪ'kruːt] (n.) 新成員；新兵
81 treason ['triːzən] (n.) 叛國；不忠；背信
82 malice ['mælɪs] (n.) 敵意；惡意
83 levy ['levi] (n.) 徵收（稅）；召集（兵）

Act 5, Scene 1
Lady Macbeth. Yet here's a spot.
Doctor. Hark! she speaks.

27 While these things were acting, the queen, who had been the sole partner in his wickedness, in whose bosom he could sometimes seek a momentary repose[84] from those terrible dreams which afflicted them both nightly, died, it is supposed, by her own hands, unable to bear the remorse[85] of guilt, and public hate; by which event he was left alone, without a soul to love or care for him, or a friend to whom he could confide[86] his wicked purposes.

84 repose [rɪˈpoʊz] (n.) 休息
85 remorse [rɪˈmɔːrs] (n.) 良心不安；懊悔
86 confide [kənˈfaɪd] (v.) 向某人傾訴

The Death of Lady Macbeth

🎧28 He grew careless of life, and wished for death; but the near approach of Malcolm's army roused[87] in him what remained of his ancient courage, and he determined to die (as he expressed it) "with armor on his back". Besides this, the hollow promises of the witches had filled him with a false confidence, and he remembered the sayings of the spirits, that none of woman born was to hurt him, and that he was never to be vanquished till Birnam wood should come to Dunsinane, which he thought could never be.

87 rouse [raʊz] (v.) 激勵

🎧 29 So he shut himself up in his castle, whose impregnable [88] strength was such as defied [89] a siege [90]: here he sullenly [91] waited the approach of Malcolm. When, upon a day, there came a messenger to him, pale and shaking with fear, almost unable to report that which he had seen; for he averred [92], that as he stood upon his watch on the hill, he looked toward Birnam, and to his thinking the wood began to move!

"Liar and slave!" cried Macbeth; "if thou speakest false, thou shalt hang alive upon the next tree, till famine [93] end thee. If thy tale be true, I care not if thou dost as much by me": for Macbeth now began to faint in resolution, and to doubt the equivocal [94] speeches of the spirits. He was not to fear till Birnam wood should come to Dunsinane; and now a wood did move!

88 impregnable [ɪmˈpregnəbəl] (a.) 不能攻下的；攻不破的
89 defy [dɪˈfaɪ] (v.) 公然反抗
90 siege [siːdʒ] (n.) 圍攻；圍困
91 sullenly [ˈsʌlənli] (adv.) 慍怒地；愁眉不展地
92 aver [əˈvɜːr] (v.)〔舊式用法〕斷言
93 famine [ˈfæmɪn] (n.) 饑荒
94 equivocal [ɪˈkwɪvəkəl] (a.) 不可靠的

🎧30 "However," said he, "if this which he avouches[95] be true, let us arm and out. There is no flying hence, nor staying here. I begin to be weary of the sun, and wish my life at an end." With these desperate speeches he sallied[96] forth upon the besiegers[97], who had now come up to the castle.

The strange appearance which had given the messenger an idea of a wood moving is easily solved. When the besieging army marched through the wood of Birnam, Malcolm, like a skilful general, instructed his soldiers to hew down everyone a bough and bear it before him, by way of concealing the true numbers of his host. This marching of the soldiers with boughs had at a distance the appearance which had frightened the messenger.

Thus were the words of the spirit brought to pass, in a sense different from that in which Macbeth had understood them and one great hold of his confidence was gone.

---

95 avouch [əˈvautʃ] (v.) 〔文學用法〕（今罕用）確言；擔保
96 sally [ˈsæli] (v.) 出擊；突圍
97 besieger [bɪˈsiːdʒər] (n.) 圍攻者

And now a severe skirmishing[98] took place, in which Macbeth, though feebly supported by those who called themselves his friends, but in reality hated the tyrant and inclined to the party of Malcolm and Macduff, yet fought with the extreme of rage and valor, cutting to pieces all who were opposed to him, till he came to where Macduff was fighting.

Seeing Macduff, and remembering the caution of the spirit who had counseled him to avoid Macduff, above all men, he would have turned, but Macduff, who had been seeking him through the whole fight, opposed his turning, and a fierce contest ensued[99]; Macduff giving him many foul reproaches for the murder of his wife and children. Macbeth, whose soul was charged enough with blood of that family already, would still have declined the combat; but Macduff still urged him to it, calling him tyrant, murderer, hellhound, and villain.

---

98 skirmish ['skɜːrmɪʃ] (n.) 小型衝突；遭遇戰
99 ensue [ɪnˈsuː] (v.) 因而發生；隨之發生

Macbeth.   Yet I will try the last. Before my body
                 I throw my warlike shield. Lay on, Macduff.

🎧 32   Then Macbeth remembered the words of the spirit, how none of woman born should hurt him; and smiling confidently he said to Macduff, "Thou losest thy labor, Macduff. As easily thou mayest impress the air with thy sword, as make me vulnerable[100]. I bear a charmed life, which must not yield to one of woman born."

---

100 vulnerable [ˈvʌlnərəbəl] (a.) 易受傷的；有弱點的

"Despair thy charm," said Macduff, "and let that lying spirit whom thou hast served, tell thee, that Macduff was never born of woman, never as the ordinary manner of men is to be born, but was untimely taken from his mother."

"Accursed[101] be the tongue which tells me so," said the trembling Macbeth, who felt his last hold of confidence

Act 5. Scene 8.

Macduff.   Turn, hellhound, turn!
Macbeth.   Of all men else I have avoided thee.
           But get thee back. My soul is too much charged
           With blood of thine already.

give way; "and let never man in future believe the lying equivocations of witches and juggling[102] spirits, who deceive us in words which have double senses, and while they keep their promise literally, disappoint our hopes with a different meaning. I will not fight with thee."

101 accursed [əˈkɜːrst] (a.) 〔詩的用法〕受詛咒的；可恨的
102 juggling [ˈdʒʌɡəlɪŋ] (a.) 誆騙的；耍把戲的

"Then live!" said the scornful Macduff; "we will have a show of thee, as men show monsters, and a painted board, on which shall be written, 'Here men may see the tyrant!'"

"Never," said Macbeth, whose courage returned with despair; "I will not live to kiss the ground before young Malcolm's feet, and to be baited[103] with the curses of the rabble[104]. Though Birnam wood be come to Dunsinane, and thou opposed to me, who wast never born of woman, yet will I try the last."

With these frantic[105] words he threw himself upon Macduff, who, after a severe struggle, in the end overcame him, and cutting off his head, made a present of it to the young and lawful king, Malcolm; who took upon him the government which, by the machinations[106] of the usurper[107], he had so long been deprived of, and ascended the throne of Duncan the Meek, amid the acclamations[108] of the nobles and the people.

---

103 bait [beɪt] (v.) 以辱罵的言語奚落某人
104 rabble ['ræbəl] (n.) 〔輕蔑用法〕下層階級的人民
105 frantic ['fræntɪk] (a.) 發狂似的；狂亂的
106 machination [ˌmækə'neɪʃən] (n.) 陰謀；策劃
107 usurper [juː'zɜːrpər] (n.) 篡位者；篡奪者
108 acclamation [ˌæklə'meɪʃən] (n.) 歡呼；喝采（常用複數形）

Quotation
MACBETH

Lady Macbeth　Yet do I fear thy nature,
　　　　　　　　It is too full o' th' milk of human kindness
　　　　　　　　To catch the nearest way. (I, v, 16-18)

馬克白夫人　但我真擔心你的天性；
　　　　　　充滿過多的仁慈乳汁，
　　　　　　使你迴避最快的方法。

　　　　　　（第一幕，第五景，16-18 行）

Lady Macbeth　Come, you spirits
　　　　　　　　That tend on mortal thoughts, unsex me here,
　　　　　　　　And fill me from the crown to the toe top-full
　　　　　　　　Of direst cruelty. (I, v, 40-43)

馬克白夫人　來吧，你們這些
　　　　　　關心人類意念的妖精，讓我變成男人，
　　　　　　讓我自頂至踵全身注滿──
　　　　　　最凶殘的冷酷。

　　　　　　（第一幕，第五景，40-43 行）

Macbeth	[Looking on his hands] This is a sorry sight.
Lady Macbeth	A foolish thought, to say a sorry sight.
Macbeth	There's one did laugh in's sleep, and one cried, "Murder!"
	That they did wake each other. I stood and heard them;
	But they did say their prayers, and address'd them
	Again to sleep. (II, ii, 18-23)
馬克白	（看著自己的雙手）真是慘不忍睹。
馬克白夫人	別傻了，說什麼慘不忍睹。
馬克白	一個在夢裡大笑，一個喊著「殺人啦！」
	互相嚇醒對方。我站定聽他們的動靜；
	他們只是做禱告，叫自己
	再繼續睡覺。
	（第二幕，第二景，18-23 行）

Lady Macbeth	Why did you bring these daggers from the place?
	They must lie there. Go carry them, and smear The sleepy grooms with blood.
Macbeth	I'll go no more.
	I am afraid to think what I have done;
	Look on't again I dare not.
Lady Macbeth	Infirm of purpose!
	Give me the daggers. (II, ii, 45-50)

馬克白夫人　你怎麼把匕首拿回來？
　　　　　　把匕首留在那裡。拿回去，然後
　　　　　　把血塗在那兩個熟睡的寢宮侍從身上。
馬克白　　　我不去了！
　　　　　　我不敢回想剛才所做的事，
　　　　　　也沒膽量再去看一眼。
馬克白夫人　真是敢做不敢當！
　　　　　　把匕首給我。
　　　　　　（第二幕，第二景，45-50 行）

Macbeth　Better be with the dead
　　　　　　Whom we, to gain our peace, have sent to peace,
　　　　　　Than on the torture of the mind to lie
　　　　　　In restless ecstasy. Duncan is in his grave;
　　　　　　After life's fitful fever he sleeps well. (III, ii, 19-23)
馬克白　　　為了我們自身的安寧，
　　　　　　我們送人去永息，
　　　　　　與其內心的折磨永無止息，
　　　　　　寧可和死人在一塊。鄧肯進了墳墓，
　　　　　　歷經人生一場場的熱病後，他正安睡著。
　　　　　　（第三幕，第二景，19-23 行）

Witches　Double, double, toil and trouble
　　　　　　Fire burn, and cauldron bubble. (IV, i, 10-11)
三女巫　　　不憚辛勞不憚煩，
　　　　　　釜中沸沫泛沸泡。
　　　　　　（第四幕，第一景，10-11 行）

Macbeth Tomorrow, and tomorrow, and tomorrow,
Creeps in this petty pace from day to day,
To the last syllable of recorded time;
And all our yesterdays have lighted fools
The way to dusty death. Out, out, brief candle!
Life's but a walking shadow, a poor player,
That struts and frets his hour upon the stage,
And then is heard no more. It is a tale
Told by an idiot, full of sound and fury
Signifying nothing. (V, v, 19-28)

馬克白　明日明日復明日，
日日躓著碎步行，
直到時間之盡頭；
我們昨日之種種，照亮傻子
奔赴黃泉的塵煙漫漫路。
熄滅吧，熄滅吧，短促的燭光！
生命不過是遊蕩的幽魂，
不過是個拙劣的伶人，
在舞台上趾高氣昂，焦躁不安，
又在無聲無息中悄然退下。這是一個
呆子所講的故事，充斥喧鬧憤怒，
卻毫無意義。
（第五幕，第五景，19-28 行）

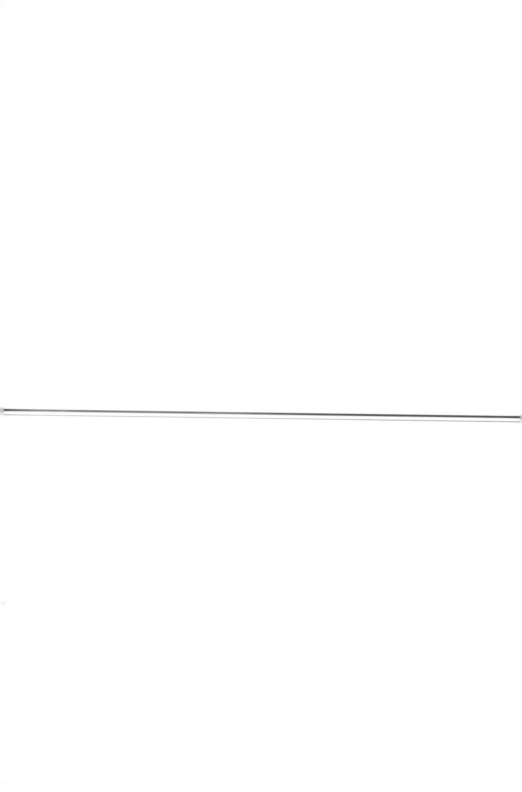

King Lear

李爾王

導讀

故事的來源

此劇最初以《李爾王的歷史》（*The History of King Lear*）為題，於 1608 年以四開本（quarto）印行，與 1623 年出版的莎翁全集對開本（the First Folio）裡的《李爾王的悲劇》（*The Tragedy of King Lear*）不同。現今有些學者認為莎士比亞先寫了 1608 年的版本，後來才修改成 1623 年的演出文本，也就是我們目前所熟知的《李爾王》。根據推測，《李爾王》完成的時間約於 1604-5 年，在《哈姆雷特》與《奧賽羅》之後、《馬克白》之前，正是處於莎士比亞撰寫悲劇的顛峰時期。

《李爾王》的故事來源有好幾個，分別是：

1136 年的《不列顛帝王史》（*Historia Regum Britanniae*）
Raphael Holinshed 的《編年史》（*Holinshed's Chronicles*, 1587）
John Higgin 的《吏鏡》（*Mirror for Magistrates*, 1574）
Edmund Spenser 於 1590 年出版的《仙后》（*Faerie Queene*）

除此之外，甚至還可能包括一樁發生在 1603 年底的訴訟案件。在 1603 年的這樁民事案件中，艾斯里爵士（Sir Brian Annesley）的兩個女兒企圖透過法律，證明老父已經失去理智，以藉此圖謀地產，但最小的女兒竭力為父親辯護。

這個小女兒叫蔻蒂兒（Cordell），與《李爾王》故事中三女兒名字相似。然而《李爾王》最重要來源的應該算是 1590 年初完成、1605 年出版的《黎爾王與三個女兒的史實》（*The True Chronicle History of King Leir and His Three Daughters*），據考證，莎士比亞在這齣戲裡，還可能演出過相當於忠臣肯特的角色。

至上的王權

王權在文藝復興時期是神聖至上的力量，國王有權力要求臣民服從尊崇他。莎士比亞在世時，舞台上就時常出現服從威權的舉止動作，如下跪和鞠躬，藉此表示對位階、財富、權力、年齡等的敬重。詹姆士王朝的英國更是注重敬老尊賢的觀念，當時的人認為這是上帝的意旨，是自然界的秩序，權力理所當然應該歸給長者。人們認為長者應嚴密控制財產，並得以懲罰作為威脅，以免權力地位被年輕人所奪。也因此，國王會不斷舉行展示王權的儀式，使得民間也顯出一片肅穆緊張的氣氛。

李爾王便是這樣一位國王，他不僅將自己的權力運用於政務，也運用在家務上。他一出場就命令女兒說出對自己的愛，當他在聽到小女兒逆耳的答覆後，為了維持尊嚴權威，他罔視公平正義，取消小女兒的繼承權。不料大女兒和二女兒在獲得權位之後，卻對老父恩斷義絕，使得失卻王權的李爾備嚐辛酸冷暖，終至精神崩潰。

LEAR

父女至親的情感

有些評論家認為《黎爾王》的開場較《李爾王》來得合理。黎爾王沒有子嗣，想找乘龍快婿，他要求三個女兒聽從他的意見來選擇丈夫。小女兒卻表示她不會嫁給父親為鞏固王權而為她挑選的丈夫，因為她不嫁自己不愛的男人。黎爾一氣之下，便將國土分給其他兩個女兒，然後退位。莎翁的《李爾王》則傳達出另一種訊息：李爾王要女兒們說出對父親的愛，透露出李爾王這種怪異心態和專斷獨裁之間的深層關

係。有人認為造成李爾王悲劇的根源是國土分配，劇中表現出許多原型的家庭關係：手足的敵對意識、失去父母寵愛的恐懼、父母害怕子女冷漠無情等等。

國王只是一種身分，李爾希望的無非是能得到女兒對父親的敬愛與尊重，但父女之間的誤會卻讓整齣劇走向難以彌補的悲劇。李爾缺乏自我認知，聽信讒言，不接受批評，一直到飽嚐恥辱痛苦之後，才開始認識到自己。

愚人一角的笑談，則預示了李爾的災難。文藝復興時期的觀眾對愚人這種角色並不陌生，愚人的嘲諷揶揄總帶有弦外之音，隱含著智慧或真理。愚人暗示的道理是：承受苦痛，比在真實世界中自以為是來得好。發瘋的李爾最後就體會到自己必須受苦才能看到真相。

兩極化的評價

近四個世紀以來，《李爾王》受到兩極化的評價。英國詩人及劇作家泰特（Nahum Tate, 1652-1715）曾在 1681 年將此劇改編為截然不同的版本，劇中刪除了愚人一角，蔻蒂莉也沒有死，李爾恢復了王位，最終以喜劇收場。

這個版本甫一推出，便受到觀眾與讀者的喜愛而風行了 153 年。一直到十九世紀中葉，人們才再度重拾原作，感受劇中生命的脆弱、人情的荒蕪、情緒的騷亂，並讚揚這齣壯闊悲涼的劇作。此後對《李爾王》的溢美之詞有增無減，甚至超越了《哈姆雷特》，將此劇奉為莎士比亞最偉大的悲劇，雪萊則認為《李爾王》是最偉大的戲劇詩作。

儘管如此，熱愛《李爾王》的讀者觀眾在讚賞此劇之餘，也不免不安。除了痛苦不堪的結局之外，本劇還有許多批評，例如，十八世紀的莎劇編輯強生（Samuel Johnson）指出李爾的行為「不可思議」；英國詩人柯立芝（Samuel Taylor Coleridge）認為劇情「顯著荒謬」，而本系列書的編撰者查爾斯‧蘭姆甚至說：「李爾根本不可能呈現於舞台上。」「看到李爾一個老人拄著枴杖，在傾盆大雨的夜晚，被女兒拒於門外，只好站在台上蹣跚而行，此景呈現的除了痛苦和嫌惡，別無他物。」

二十世紀著名的莎劇評論家卜瑞黎（A. C. Bradley）在提到《李爾王》時，更是開門見山地提出一個問題：「為何此劇受到眾人熱烈的褒揚，又受封為莎士比亞最偉大的悲劇，可是卻是四大悲劇中最不受歡迎的一齣呢？」

KING LEAR.

Lear — Blow, winds, & crack your cheeks!

Act 3   Scene 2

卜瑞黎對這些反應的答覆是：「《李爾王》是莎士比亞最偉大的成就，卻不是他最好的劇作。」從劇本的角度來看，《李爾王》比其他三齣悲劇略遜一籌。如果不從劇本的角度來看，《李爾王》卻「完全顯露了莎士比亞的力量，就如同但丁的《神曲》或貝多芬壯闊的交響曲一般」，唯一的缺憾是「舞台上容不下這種大戲。」

英國文學家韓茲黎（William Hazlitt）形容，此劇「像海洋般洶湧、狂囂、怒號，沒有邊際、沒有希望、沒有燈塔、也沒有錨」，只能在心靈與想像的劇場中演出。這或許就如卜瑞黎所言：「我們得棄絕、痛恨這個世界，含笑拋棄這個世界，因為最真實的只有靈魂，靈魂包含了勇氣、耐心與奉獻，沒有任何外在的東西可以碰觸得到。」

李爾學習到珍貴的教訓，並不代表他獲得了救贖。令人驚怖的結局讓人懷疑正義公理何在，為何所有正直美好的價值觀在這齣戲中都顯得顛倒錯亂？在莎士比亞所有的戲劇中，沒有一齣像《李爾王》一樣，讓不公不義如此暴虐囂張又無需受到懲罰。然而這齣悲劇並非漠視邪惡、愚蠢及痛苦，而是要我們正視這些陰暗面，看清人類的邪惡如何使人萬劫不復，又如何在苦痛中展現愛的力量。

另外，善於改編莎劇的英國導演布魯克（Peter Brook）於 1970 年執導電影《李爾王》，影片根據原作加以刪減及改編，呈現出二十世紀的觀點，被許多人認為是目前最好的改編版本。有興趣的讀者不妨參考之。

人物表

King Lear	李爾王	故事的男主人翁，不列顛國王
Cordelia	蔻蒂莉	李爾王的小女兒
Goneril	葛奈麗	李爾王的大女兒
Regan	麗晶	李爾王的二女兒
King of France	法國國王	三女兒蔻蒂莉之夫
Duke of Albany	歐伯尼公爵	大女兒葛奈麗之夫
Duke of Cornwall	康沃公爵	二女兒麗晶之夫
Earl of Kent	肯特伯爵	李爾王的忠臣，後化名為「凱爾斯」（Caius）
Fool	愚者	李爾王的弄臣
Earl of Gloucester	葛勞賽斯特伯爵	艾德蒙（Edmund），將蔻蒂莉害死獄中

King Lear

Lear, King of Britain, had three daughters; Goneril, wife to the Duke of Albany; Regan, wife to the Duke of Cornwall; and Cordelia, a young maid, for whose love the King of France and Duke of Burgundy were joint suitors, and were at this time making stay for that purpose in the court of Lear.

The old king, worn out with age and the fatigues of government, he being more than fourscore years old, determined to take no further part in state affairs, but to leave the management to younger strengths, that he might have time to prepare for death, which must at no long period ensue.

🎧36 With this intent he called his three daughters to him, to know from their own lips which of them loved him best, that he might part his kingdom among them in such proportions[1] as their affection for him should seem to deserve.

Goneril, the eldest, declared that she loved her father more than words could give out, that he was dearer to her than the light of her own eyes, dearer than life and liberty, with a deal of such professing[2] stuff, which is easy to counterfeit[3] where there is no real love, only a few fine words delivered with confidence being wanted in that case.

The king, delighted to hear from her own mouth this assurance of her love, and thinking truly that her heart went with it, in a fit of fatherly fondness bestowed[4] upon her and her husband one third of his ample kingdom.

1 proportions [prə'pɔːrʃənz] (n.) 大小;面積(作複數形)
2 professing [prə'fesɪŋ] (a.) 聲稱的;自稱的
3 counterfeit ['kaʊntəfɪtər] (v.) 偽造;仿造
4 bestow [bɪ'stoʊ] (v.) 賜贈

🎧37 Then calling to him his second daughter, he demanded what she had to say. Regan, who was made of the same hollow metal as her sister, was not a whit[5] behind in her professions, but rather declared that what her sister had spoken came short of the love which she professed to bear for his highness; insomuch that she found all other joys dead, in comparison with the pleasure which she took in the love of her dear king and father.

Lear blessed himself in having such loving children, as he thought; and could do no less, after the handsome assurances which Regan had made, than bestow a third of his kingdom upon her and her husband, equal in size to that which he had already given away to Goneril.

Then turning to his youngest daughter Cordelia, whom he called his joy, he asked what she had to say, thinking no doubt that she would glad his ears with the same loving speeches which her sisters had uttered, or rather that her expressions would be so much stronger than theirs, as she had always been his darling, and favored by him above either of them.

5 whit [wɪt] (n.) (多用於否定句) 絲毫

🎧38   But Cordelia, disgusted with the flattery of her sisters, whose hearts she knew were far from their lips, and seeing that all their coaxing[6] speeches were only intended to wheedle[7] the old king out of his dominions[8], that they and their husbands might reign in his lifetime, made no other reply but this— that she loved his majesty according to her duty, neither more nor less.

The king, shocked with this appearance of ingratitude[9] in his favorite child, desired her to consider her words, and to mend her speech, lest it should mar[10] her fortunes.

Cordelia then told her father, that he was her father, that he had given her breeding, and loved her; that she returned those duties back as was most fit, and did obey him, love him, and most honor him. But that she could not frame her mouth to such large speeches as her sisters had done, or promise to love nothing else in the world.

6 coaxing [ˈkoʊksɪŋ] (a.) 哄誘的；勸誘的
7 wheedle [ˈwiːdl] (v.) 諂媚；哄騙
8 dominion [dəˈmɪnjən] (n.) 領土；版圖
9 ingratitude [ɪnˈɡrætɪtuːd] (n.) 忘恩負義
10 mar [mɑːr] (v.) 毀損；損傷；玷污

🎧39 Why had her sisters husbands, if (as they said) they had no love for anything but their father? If she should ever wed, she was sure the lord to whom she gave her hand would want half her love, half of her care and duty; she should never marry like her sisters, to love her father all.

Cordelia, who in earnest loved her old father even almost as extravagantly[11] as her sisters pretended to do, would have plainly told him so at any other time, in more daughter-like and loving terms, and without these qualifications, which did indeed sound a little ungracious[12]; but after the crafty flattering speeches of her sisters, which she had seen draw such extravagant rewards, she thought the handsomest thing she could do was to love and be silent. This put her affection out of suspicion of mercenary[13] ends, and showed that she loved, but not for gain; and that her professions, the less ostentatious[14] they were, had so much the more of truth and sincerity than her sisters'.

11 extravagantly [ɪkˈstrævəgəntli] (adv.) 揮霍無度地
12 ungracious [ʌnˈgreɪʃəs] (a.) 不客氣的
13 mercenary [ˈmɜːrsəneri] (a.) 愛財所致的；圖利的
14 ostentatious [ˌɑːstənˈteɪʃəs] (a.) 好誇耀的；招搖的

🎧40 This plainness of speech, which Lear called pride, so enraged the old monarch—who in his best of times always showed much of spleen[15] and rashness, and in whom the dotage[16] incident to old age had so clouded over his reason, that he could not discern[17] truth from flattery, nor a gay painted speech from words that came from the heart—that in a fury of resentment[18] he retracted[19] the third part of his kingdom which yet remained, and which he had reserved for Cordelia, and gave it away from her, sharing it equally between her two sisters and their husbands, the Dukes of Albany and Cornwall; whom he now called to him, and in presence of all his courtiers bestowing a coronet[20] between them, invested them jointly with all the power, revenue, and execution of government, only retaining to himself the name of king; all the rest of royalty he resigned; with this reservation, that himself, with a hundred knights for his attendants, was to be maintained by monthly course in each of his daughters' palaces in turn.

15 spleen [spliːn] (n.) 壞脾氣；憤怒
16 dotage ['doʊtɪdʒ] (n.) 因年老而心力衰退
17 discern [dɪ'sɜːrn] (v.) (用眼或用心)明辨
18 resentment [rɪ'zentmənt] (n.) 憤慨；怨恨
19 retract [riː'trækt] (v.) 收回；撤回
20 coronet [ˌkɑːrə'net] (n.) 貴族所戴的小冠冕

🎧 So preposterous[21] a disposal of his kingdom, so little guided by reason, and so much by passion, filled all his courtiers with astonishment and sorrow; but none of them had the courage to interpose[22] between this incensed[23] king and his wrath, except the Earl of Kent, who was beginning to speak a good word for Cordelia, when the passionate Lear on pain of death commanded him to desist[24]; but the good Kent was not so to be repelled[25].

---

21 preposterous [prɪ'pɑːstərəs] (a.) 荒謬的；反常的
22 interpose [ˌɪntər'pouz] (v.) 介入……之間；調停
23 incensed ['ɪnsensd] (a.) 被激怒的
24 desist [dɪ'sɪst] (v.) 〔正式用法〕停止
25 repel [rɪ'pel] (v.) 逐退；驅開

LEAR, KENT, AND FOOL

He had been ever loyal to Lear, whom he had honored as a king, loved as a father, followed as a master; and he had never esteemed his life further than as a pawn[26] to wage[27] against his royal master's enemies, nor feared to lose it when Lear's safety was the motive; nor now that Lear was most his own enemy, did this faithful servant of the king forget his old principles, but manfully[28] opposed Lear, to do Lear good; and was unmannerly only because Lear was mad.

26 pawn [pɑ:n] (n.) 兵;卒（棋盤中份量最輕的棋子）
27 wage [weɪdʒ] (v.) 進行戰役或活動
28 manfully ['mænfəli] (adv.) 勇敢地;堅決地

【43】 He had been a most faithful counselor in times
past to the king, and he besought[29] him now, that
he would see with his eyes (as he had done in many
weighty matters), and go by his advice still; and in
his best consideration recall this hideous rashness:
for he would answer with his life, his judgment that
Lear's youngest daughter did not love him least, nor
were those empty-hearted whose low sound gave no
token[30] of hollowness.

When power bowed to flattery, honor was bound to
plainness. For Lear's threats, what could he do to him,
whose life was already at his service? That should not
hinder duty from speaking.

The honest freedom of this good Earl of Kent
only stirred up the king's wrath the more, and like a
frantic patient who kills his physician, and loves his
mortal disease, he banished[31] this true servant, and
allotted[32] him but five days to make his preparations
for departure; but if on the sixth his hated person was
found within the realm of Britain, that moment was to
be his death.

29 beseech [bɪ'siːtʃ] (n.) 懇求
30 token ['toʊkən] (n.) 標誌；象徵
31 banish ['bænɪʃ] (v.) 放逐；驅逐出境
32 allot [ə'lɑːt] (v.) 分配；指派

And Kent bade farewell to the king, and said, that since he chose to show himself in such fashion, it was but banishment to stay there; and before he went, he recommended Cordelia to the protection of the gods, the maid who had so rightly thought, and so discreetly[33] spoken; and only wished that her sisters' large speeches might be answered with deeds of love; and then he went, as he said, to shape his old course to a new country.

The King of France and Duke of Burgundy were now called in to hear the determination of Lear about his youngest daughter, and to know whether they would persist in their courtship to Cordelia, now that she was under her father's displeasure, and had no fortune but her own person to recommend her.

33 discreetly [dɪˈskriːtli] (adv.) 謹慎地；考慮周到地

And the Duke of Burgundy declined the match, and would not take her to wife upon such conditions; but the King of France, understanding what the nature of the fault had been which had lost her the love of her father, that it was only a tardiness[34] of speech, and the not being able to frame her tongue to flattery like her sisters,

Cordelia. Who cover faults, at last shame them derides.
Well may you prosper!
King of France. Come, my fair Cordelia.   Act 1. Scene 1.

took this young maid by the hand, and saying that her virtues were a dowry[35] above a kingdom, bade Cordelia to take farewell of her sisters and of her father, though he had been unkind, and she should go with him, and be queen of him and of fair France, and reign over fairer possessions than her sisters.

---

34 tardiness ['tɑːrdɪnəs] (n.) 緩慢
35 dowry ['daʊri] (n.) 嫁妝

And he called the Duke of Burgundy in contempt a waterish duke, because his love for this young maid had in a moment run all away like water.

Then Cordelia with weeping eyes took leave of her sisters, and besought them to love their father well, and make good their professions: and they sullenly told her not to prescribe to them, for they knew their duty; but to strive to content her husband, who had taken her (as they tauntingly[36] expressed it) as Fortune's alms[37].

And Cordelia with a heavy heart departed, for she knew the cunning of her sisters, and she wished her father in better hands than she was about to leave him in.

36 tauntingly ['tɔːntɪnli] (adv.) 辱罵地；奚落地
37 alms [ɑːmz] (n.) 救濟金；救濟品

🎧47 Cordelia was no sooner gone, than the devilish dispositions of her sisters began to show themselves in their true colors. Even before the expiration of the first month, which Lear was to spend by agreement with his eldest daughter Goneril, the old king began to find out the difference between promises and performances.

This wretch having got from her father all that he had to bestow, even to the giving away of the crown from off his head, began to grudge[38] even those small remnants[39] of royalty which the old man had reserved to himself, to please his fancy with the idea of being still a king.

---

38 grudge [grʌdʒ] (v.) 怨恨；妒忌
39 remnants [ˈremnənts] (n.) 剩下的殘餘物（作複數形）

48 She could not bear to see him and his hundred knights. Every time she met her father, she put on a frowning countenance[40]; and when the old man wanted to speak with her, she would feign[41] sickness, or anything to get rid of the sight of him; for it was plain that she esteemed his old age a useless burden, and his attendants an unnecessary expense: not only she herself slackened[42] in her expressions of duty to the king, but by her example, and (it is to be feared) not without her private instructions her very servants affected to treat him with neglect, and would either refuse to obey his orders, or still more contemptuously pretend not to hear them.

40 countenance ['kaʊntɪnəns] (n.) 面色；容貌
41 feign [feɪn] (v.) 假裝
42 slacken ['slækən] (v.) 使緩慢遲滯；變得不景氣

🎧49 Lear could not but perceive this alteration in the behavior of his daughter, but he shut his eyes against it as long as he could, as people commonly are unwilling to believe the unpleasant consequences which their own mistakes and obstinacy[43] have brought upon them.

True love and fidelity[44] are no more to be estranged by ill, than falsehood and hollow-heartedness can be conciliated by good usage. This eminently[45] appears in the instance of the good Earl of Kent, who, though banished by Lear, and his life made forfeit[46] if he were found in Britain, chose to stay and abide[47] all consequences, as long as there was a chance of his being useful to the king his master.

---

43 obstinacy ['ɔːbstɪnəsi] (n.) 頑固；頑強
44 fidelity [fɪ'deləti] (n.) 忠誠；忠貞
45 eminently ['emɪnəntli] (adv.) 性質優良地
46 forfeit ['fɔːrfit] (a.)〔文學用法〕因受罰而喪失的
47 abide [ə'baɪd] (v.)〔文學用法〕等待

🎧(50) See to what mean shifts and disguises poor loyalty is forced to submit[48] sometimes; yet it counts nothing base[49] or unworthy, so as it can but do service where it owes an obligation!

In the disguise of a serving man, all his greatness and pomp[50] laid aside, this good earl proffered[51] his services to the king, who, not knowing him to be Kent in that disguise, but pleased with a certain plainness, or rather bluntness[52] in his answers, which the earl put on (so different from that smooth oily flattery which he had so much reason to be sick of, having found the effects not answerable in his daughter), a bargain was quickly struck, and Lear took Kent into his service by the name of Caius, as he called himself, never suspecting him to be his once great favorite, the high and mighty Earl of Kent.

48 submit [səb'mɪt] (v.) 投降;使屈服
49 base [beɪs] (a.) （指人的思想行為）卑鄙的
50 pomp [pɑːmp] (n.) 壯觀;盛況
51 proffer ['prɑːfər] (v.) 提出;提供
52 bluntness ['blʌntnəs] (n.) 直率;直言

This Caius quickly found means to show his fidelity and love to his royal master: for Goneril's steward that same day behaving in a disrespectful manner to Lear, and giving him saucy[53] looks and language, as no doubt he was secretly encouraged to do by his mistress,

Caius, not enduring to hear so open an affront[54] put upon his majesty, made no more ado[55] but presently tripped up his heels, and laid the unmannerly slave in the kennel[56]; for which friendly service Lear became more and more attached to him.

53 saucy ['sɑːsi] (a.) 無禮的；莽撞的
54 affront [əˈfrʌnt] (n.) 公然侮辱；故意表示不敬
55 ado [əˈduː] (n.)〔古代用法〕無謂的紛擾
56 kennel [ˈkenl] (n.) 飼養獵犬場；狗房

Nor was Kent the only friend Lear had. In his degree, and as far as so insignificant a personage[57] could show his love, the poor fool, or jester[58], that had been of his palace while Lear had a palace, as it was the custom of kings and great personages at that time to keep a fool (as he was called) to make them sport after serious business: this poor fool

clung to Lear after he had given away his crown, and by his witty sayings would keep up his good humor, though he could not refrain[59] sometimes from jeering[60] at his master for his imprudence[61] in uncrowning himself, and giving all away to his daughters; at which time, as he rhymingly expressed it, these daughters

---

57 personage ['pɜːrsənɪdʒ] (n.) 顯要；大人物
58 jester ['dʒestər] (n.) 古時宮廷或貴族的弄臣
59 refrain [rɪ'freɪn] (v.) 抑制；克制
60 jeer [dʒɪr] (v.) 嘲笑；奚落
61 imprudence [ɪm'pruːdəns] (n.) 輕率；不謹慎

For sudden joy did weep
  And he for sorrow sung,
That such a king should play bo-peep[62]
  And go the fools among.

And in such wild sayings, and scraps[63] of songs, of which he had plenty, this pleasant honest fool poured out his heart even in the presence of Goneril herself, in many a bitter taunt[64] and jest which cut to the quick: such as comparing the king to the hedge-sparrow, who feeds the young of the cuckoo till they grow old enough, and then has its head bit off for its pains; and saying, that an ass may know when the cart[65] draws the horse (meaning that Lear's daughters, that ought to go behind, now ranked before their father); and, that Lear was no longer Lear, but the shadow of Lear: for which free speeches he was once or twice threatened to be whipped[66].

---

62 bo-peep [bouˈpiːp] (n.) 躲貓貓遊戲
63 scrap [skræp] (n.) 碎片；小塊；少量
64 taunt [tɔːnt] (n.) 辱罵；嘲笑；奚落
65 cart [kɑːrt] (n.) 二輪單馬車
66 whip [wɪp] (v.) 鞭打

The coolness and falling off of respect which Lear had begun to perceive, were not all which this foolish fond father was to suffer from his unworthy daughter: she now plainly told him that his staying in her palace was inconvenient so long as he insisted upon keeping up an establishment of a hundred knights; that this establishment was useless and expensive, and only served to fill her court with riot[67] and feasting; and she prayed him that he would lessen their number, and keep none but old men about him, such as himself, and fitting his age.

Lear at first could not believe his eyes or ears, nor that it was his daughter who spoke so unkindly. He could not believe that she who had received a crown from him could seek to cut off his train, and grudge him the respect due to his old age.

But she, persisting in her undutiful demand, the old man's rage was so excited, that he called her a detested[68] kite, and said that she spoke an untruth; and so indeed she did, for the hundred knights were all men of choice behavior and sobriety[69] of manners, skilled in all particulars of duty, and not given to rioting or feasting, as she said.

---

67 riot [ˈraɪət] (n.) 放肆的行為；狂歡
68 detested [dɪˈtestɪd] (a.) 令人深恨的
69 sobriety [səˈbraɪəti] (n.) 自制；嚴肅

Act 1. Scene 4.

Lear.   Hear, Nature, hear! dear goddess, hear!
Suspend thy purpose, if thou didst intend
To make this creature fruitful!

🎧 55 And he bid his horses to be prepared, for he would go to his other daughter, Regan, he and his hundred knights; and he spoke of ingratitude, and said it was a marble-hearted devil, and showed more hideous in a child than the sea-monster.

And he cursed his eldest daughter Goneril so as was terrible to hear; praying that she might never have a child, or if she had, that it might live to return that scorn[70] and contempt upon her which she had shown to him: that she might feel how sharper than a serpent's tooth it was to have a thankless child.

And Goneril's husband, the Duke of Albany, beginning to excuse himself for any share which Lear might suppose he had in the unkindness, Lear would not hear him out, but in a rage ordered his horses to be saddled[71], and set out with his followers for the abode[72] of Regan, his other daughter.

70 scorn [skɔːrn] (n.) 輕蔑；藐視
71 saddle [ˈsædl] (v.) 裝上馬鞍
72 abode [əˈboud] (n.)〔舊時用法〕〔文學用法〕住所；房屋

Act 1. Scene 5.

Lear.　Go you before to Gloucester with these letters.

🎧 56 And Lear thought to himself how small the fault of Cordelia (if it was a fault) now appeared, in comparison with her sister's, and he wept; and then he was ashamed that such a creature as Goneril should have so much power over his manhood as to make him weep.

Regan and her husband were keeping their court in great pomp and state at their palace; and Lear despatched[73] his servant Caius with letters to his daughter, that she might be prepared for his reception, while he and his train followed after.

73 despatch [dɪˈspætʃ] (v.) 派遣

But it seems that Goneril had been beforehand with him, sending letters also to Regan, accusing her father of waywardness[74] and ill humors, and advising her not to receive so great a train as he was bringing with him.

This messenger arrived at the same time with Caius, and Caius and he met: and who should it be but Caius's old enemy the steward, whom he had formerly tripped up by the heels for his saucy behavior to Lear.

Caius not liking the fellow's look, and suspecting what he came for, began to revile[75] him, and challenged him to fight, which the fellow refusing, Caius, in a fit of honest passion, beat him soundly, as such a mischief-maker and carrier of wicked messages deserved; which coming to the ears of Regan and her husband, they ordered Caius to be put in the stocks[76], though he was a messenger from the king her father, and in that character demanded the highest respect.

[74] waywardness ['weɪwərdnəs] (n.) 任性；剛愎
[75] revile [rɪ'vaɪl] (v.) 辱罵；謾罵
[76] stocks [stɑːks] (n.) 足械（一種刑具，作複數形）

58 So that the first thing the king saw when he entered the castle, was his faithful servant Caius sitting in that disgraceful situation.

This was but a bad omen[77] of the reception which he was to expect; but a worse followed, when, upon inquiry for his daughter and her husband, he was told they were weary with traveling all night, and could not see him; and when lastly, upon his insisting in a positive and angry manner to see them, they came to greet him, whom should he see in their company but the hated Goneril, who had come to tell her own story, and set her sister against the king her father!

77 omen [ˈoʊmən] (n.) 徵兆

Act 2. Scene 4.

Lear.　　　O Regan, wilt thou take her by the hand?
Goneril.　Why not by th' hand, sir? How have I offended?

🎧 59 This sight much moved the old man, and still more to see Regan take her by the hand; and he asked Goneril if she was not ashamed to look upon his old white beard. And Regan advised him to go home again with Goneril, and live with her peaceably, dismissing half of his attendants, and to ask her forgiveness; for he was old and wanted discretion, and must be ruled and led by persons that had more discretion than himself.

🎧 60 And Lear showed how preposterous that would sound, if he were to go down on his knees, and beg of his own daughter for food and raiment[78], and he argued against such an unnatural dependence, declaring his resolution never to return with her, but to stay where he was with Regan, he and his hundred knights; for he said that she had not forgot the half of the kingdom which he had endowed[79] her with, and that her eyes were not fierce like Goneril's, but mild and kind. And he said that rather than return to Goneril, with half his train cut off, he would go over to France, and beg a wretched pension[80] of the king there, who had married his youngest daughter without a portion.

But he was mistaken in expecting kinder treatment of Regan than he had experienced from her sister Goneril. As if willing to outdo her sister in unfilial[81] behavior, she declared that she thought fifty knights too many to wait upon him: that five-and-twenty were enough.

78 raiment ['reɪmənt] (n.) 〔文學用法〕衣服
79 endow [ɪn'daʊ] (v.) 捐贈
80 pension ['penʃən] (n.) 養老金
81 unfilial [ʌn'fɪliəl] (a.) 不孝的

Then Lear, nigh[82] heartbroken, turned to Goneril and said that he would go back with her, for her fifty doubled five-and-twenty, and so her love was twice as much as Regan's.

But Goneril excused herself, and said, what need of so many as five-and twenty? or even ten? or five? when he might be waited upon by her servants, or her sister's servants?

So these two wicked daughters, as if they strove to exceed each other in cruelty to their old father, who had been so good to them, by little and little would have abated[83] him of all his train, all respect (little enough for him that once commanded a kingdom), which was left him to show that he had once been a king!

Not that a splendid train is essential to happiness, but from a king to a beggar is a hard change, from commanding millions to be without one attendant; and it was the ingratitude in his daughters' denying it, more than what he would suffer by the want of it, which pierced this poor king to the heart.

82 nigh [naɪ] (adv.) 〔古代用法〕〔詩的用法〕靠近
83 abate [əˈbeɪt] (v.) 減少

🎧 62 Insomuch that with this double ill-usage, and vexation[84] for having so foolishly given away a kingdom, his wits began to be unsettled, and while he said he knew not what, he vowed revenge against those unnatural hags[85], and to make examples of them that should be a terror to the earth!

---

84 vexation [vekˈseɪʃən] (n.) 令人惱怒的事物
85 hag [hæg] (n.) 女巫；兇惡的醜老太婆

🎧 **63**   While he was thus idly threatening what his weak arm could never execute[86], night came on, and a loud storm of thunder and lightning with rain; and his daughters still persisting in their resolution not to admit his followers, he called for his horses, and chose rather to encounter the utmost fury of the storm abroad, than stay under the same roof with these ungrateful daughters: and they, saying that the injuries which wilful men procure[87] to themselves are their just punishment, suffered him to go in that condition and shut their doors upon him.

The winds were high, and the rain and storm increased, when the old man sallied forth to combat with the elements, less sharp than his daughters' unkindness.

---

86 execute ['eksɪkjuːt] (v.) 實施；執行
87 procure [proʊ'kjʊr] (v.)〔舊時用法〕促成；引致

🎧 64 For many miles about there was scarce a bush; and there upon a heath, exposed to the fury of the storm in a dark night, did King Lear wander out, and defy[88] the winds and the thunder; and he bid the winds to blow the earth into the sea, or swell the waves of the sea till they drowned the earth, that no token might remain of any such ungrateful animal as man.

The old king was now left with no other companion than the poor fool, who still abided with him, with his merry conceits[89] striving to outjest misfortune, saying it was but a naughty night to swim in, and truly the king had better go in and ask his daughter's blessing—

But he that has a little tiny wit—
With heigh ho, the wind and the rain!
Must make content with his fortunes fit.
Though the rain it raineth every day:

and swearing it was a brave night to cool a lady's pride.

88 defy [dɪˈfaɪ] (v.) 公然反抗；聲言不惜訴諸武力
89 conceit [kənˈsiːt] (n.) 詼諧機智的思想或語句

FOOL

(sings)

He that has and a little tiny wit—

With heigh-ho, the wind and the rain—

Must make content with his fortunes fit,

For the rain it raineth every day.

Act 3. Scene 2.

🎧65 Thus poorly accompanied, this once great monarch was found by his ever-faithful servant the good Earl of Kent, now transformed to Caius, who ever followed close at his side, though the king did not know him to be the earl; and be said, "Alas! sir, are you here? creatures that love night, love not such nights as these. This dreadful storm has driven the beasts to their hiding places. Man's nature cannot endure the affliction[90] or the fear."

And Lear rebuked[91] him and said, these lesser evils were not felt, where a greater malady[92] was fixed. When the mind is at ease, the body has leisure to be delicate, but the tempest in his mind did take all feeling else from his senses, but of that which beat at his heart.

And he spoke of filial ingratitude, and said it was all one as if the mouth should tear the hand for lifting food to it; for parents were hands and food and everything to children.

90 affliction [əˈflɪkʃən] (n.) 痛苦
91 rebuke [rɪˈbjuːk] (v.) 指責
92 malady [ˈmælədi] (n.) 疾病

But the good Caius still persisting in his entreaties that the king would not stay out in the open air, at last persuaded him to enter a little wretched hovel[93] which stood upon the heath, where the fool first entering, suddenly ran back terrified, saying that he had seen a spirit.

93 hovel ['hɑːvəl] (n.) 棚子；不適合居住的小屋

Act 5. Scene 4.

Lear. Didst thou give all to thy two daughters, and art thou come to this?
Edgar. Who gives any thing to Poor Tom?

67 But upon examination this spirit proved to be nothing more than a poor Bedlam[94] beggar, who had crept into this deserted hovel for shelter, and with his talk about devils frighted the fool: one of those poor lunatics who are either mad, or feign to be so, the better to extort[95] charity from the compassionate country people, who go about the country, calling themselves poor Tom and poor Turlygood, saying, "Who gives anything to poor Tom?" sticking pins and nails and sprigs[96] of rosemary into their arms to make them bleed; and with such horrible actions, partly by prayers, and partly with lunatic curses, they move or terrify the ignorant countryfolk into giving them alms.

94 Bedlam ['bedləm] (n.) 〔舊時用法〕瘋人院
95 extort [ɪk'stɔːrt] (v.) 以暴力威脅來獲得；強取
96 sprig [sprɪg] (n.) 有葉的小枝；嫩枝

🎧 68   This poor fellow was such a one; and the king seeing him in so wretched a plight[97], with nothing but a blanket about his loins[98] to cover his nakedness, could not be persuaded but that the fellow was some father who had given all away to his daughters, and brought himself to that pass: for nothing he thought could bring a man to such wretchedness but the having unkind daughters.

And from this and many such wild speeches which he uttered, the good Caius plainly perceived that he was not in his perfect mind, but that his daughters' ill usage had really made him go mad.

And now the loyalty of this worthy Earl of Kent showed itself in more essential services than he had hitherto found opportunity to perform.

97 plight [plaɪt] (n.) 困境
98 loins [lɔɪnz] (n.) 腰部（作複數形）

🎧 69 For with the assistance of some of the king's attendants who remained loyal, he had the person of his royal master removed at daybreak to the castle of Dover, where his own friends and influence, as Earl of Kent, chiefly lay; and himself embarking[99] for France, hastened to the court of Cordelia, and did there in such moving terms represent the pitiful condition of her royal father, and set out in such lively colors the inhumanity of her sisters, that this good and loving child with many tears besought the king her husband that he would give her leave to embark for England, with a sufficient power to subdue[100] these cruel daughters and their husbands, and restore the old king her father to his throne; which being granted, she set forth, and with a royal army landed at Dover.

99 embark [ɪmˈbɑːrk] (v.) 上船
100 subdue [səbˈduː] (v.) 征服；克服；壓制

Lear having by some chance escaped from the guardians which the good Earl of Kent had put over him to take care of him in his lunacy, was found by some of Cordelia's train, wandering about the fields near Dover, in a pitiable condition, stark[101] mad, and singing aloud to himself, with a crown upon his head which, he had made of straw, and nettles[102], and other wild weeds that he had picked up in the cornfields.

By the advice of the physicians, Cordelia, though earnestly desirous of seeing her father, was prevailed upon to put off the meeting, till by sleep and the operation of herbs which they gave him, he should be restored to greater composure[103].

101 stark [stɑːrk] (a.) 完全的；純然的
102 nettle ['netl] (n.) 蕁麻
103 composure [kəm'poʊʒər] (n.) 心神鎮定；泰然自若

71 By the aid of these skilful physicians, to whom Cordelia promised all her gold and jewels for the recovery of the old king, Lear was soon in a condition to see his daughter.

A tender sight it was to see the meeting between this father and daughter; to see the struggles between the joy of this poor old king at beholding[104] again his once darling child, and the shame at receiving such filial kindness from her whom he had cast off for so small a fault in his displeasure; both these passions struggling with the remains of his malady, which in his half-crazed brain sometimes made him that he scarce remembered where he was, or who it was that so kindly kissed him and spoke to him.

104 behold [bɪ'hoʊld] (n.) 〔舊時用法〕〔文學用法〕注意;看(尤指不尋常或可驚之事)

73▶ And she told her father how she had come from France with purpose to bring him assistance; and he said that she must forget and forgive, for he was old and foolish, and did not know what he did; but that to be sure she had great cause not to love him, but her sisters had none. And Cordelia said that she had no cause, no more than they had.

So we will leave this old king in the protection of his dutiful and loving child, where, by the help of sleep and medicine, she and her physicians at length succeeded in winding up[105] the untuned and jarring[106] senses which the cruelty of his other daughters had so violently shaken.

105 wind up 結束
106 jarring [ˈdʒɑːrɪŋ] (a.) 引起不調和的

74 Let us return to say a word or two about those cruel daughters. These monsters of ingratitude, who had been so false to their old father, could not be expected to prove more faithful to their own husbands. They soon grew tired of paying even the appearance of duty and affection, and in an open way showed they had fixed their loves upon another.

It happened that the object of their guilty loves was the same. It was Edmund, a natural son of the late Earl of Gloucester, who by his treacheries had succeeded in disinheriting[107] his brother Edgar, the lawful heir, from his earldom, and by his wicked practices was now earl himself; a wicked man, and a fit object for the love of such wicked creatures as Goneril and Regan.

It falling out about this time that the Duke of Cornwall, Regan's husband, died, Regan immediately declared her intention of wedding this Earl of Gloucester, which rousing the jealousy of her sister, to whom as well as to Regan this wicked earl had at sundry[108] times professed love, Goneril found means to make away with her sister by poison.

107 disinherit [ˌdɪsɪnˈherɪt] (v.) 剝奪繼承權
108 sundry [ˈsʌndri] (a.) 各種的；多方面的

Act 3. Scene 7.

Gloucester.   What mean your graces? Good my friends, consider
              You are my guests: do me no foul play, friends.
Cornwall.   Bind him, I say.

🎧75 But being detected in her practices, and imprisoned by her husband, the Duke of Albany, for this deed, and for her guilty passion for the earl which had come to his ears, she, in a fit of disappointed love and rage, shortly put an end to her own life. Thus the justice of heaven at last overtook[109] these wicked daughters.

While the eyes of all men were upon this event, admiring the justice displayed in their deserved deaths, the same eyes were suddenly taken off from this sight to admire at the mysterious ways of the same power in the melancholy[110] fate of the young and virtuous daughter, the Lady Cordelia, whose good deeds did seem to deserve a more fortunate conclusion: but it is an awful truth, that innocence and piety are not always successful in this world.

The forces which Goneril and Regan had sent out under the command of the bad Earl of Gloucester were victorious, and Cordelia, by the practices of this wicked earl, who did not like that any should stand between him and the throne, ended her life in prison.

109 overtake [ˌoʊvərˈteɪk] (v.) （指暴風雨、麻煩等）突然降臨於某人
110 melancholy [ˈmelənkɑːli] (a.) 悲哀的；鬱悶的

76 Thus, heaven took this innocent lady to itself in her young years, after showing her to the world an illustrious[111] example of filial duty. Lear did not long survive this kind child.

111 illustrious [ɪˈlʌstrɪəs] (a.) 傑出的；著名的

Before he died, the good Earl of Kent, who had still attended his old master's steps from the first of his daughters' ill usage to this sad period of his decay, tried to make him understand that it was he who had followed him under the name of Caius; but Lear's care-crazed brain at that time could not comprehend how that could be, or how Kent and Caius could be the same person: so Kent thought it needless to trouble him with explanations at such a time; and Lear soon after expiring, this faithful servant to the king, between age and grief for his old master's vexations, soon followed him to the grave.

How the judgment of heaven overtook the bad Earl of Gloucester, whose treasons were discovered, and himself slain[112] in single combat with his brother, the lawful earl and how Goneril's husband, the Duke of Albany, who was innocent of the death of Cordelia, and had never encouraged his lady in her wicked proceedings[113] against her father, ascended the throne of Britain after the death of Lear, is needless here to narrate; Lear and his three daughters being dead, whose adventures alone concern our story.

112 slay [sleɪ] (v.) 殺;謀殺
113 proceeding [prəˈsiːdɪŋ] (n.) 做過的事;行為

King Lear If she must teem,
Create her child of spleen, that it may live
And be a thwart disnatur'd torment to her!
Let it stamp wrinkles in her brow of youth,
With cadent tears fret channels in her cheeks,
Turn all her mother's pains and benefits
To laughter and contempt, that she may feel
How sharper than a serpent's tooth it is
To have a thankless child. (IV, iv, 281-89)

李爾王 如果她必得生子，
就給她生個孽子，
讓她終身都受苦！
在她年輕的額角刻上皺紋，
在她雙頰劃出一道道淚痕；
教她鞠育的辛勞；
徒換來冷笑白眼；
讓她也知道一個負心的孩子，
比毒蛇的牙更讓人痛入骨髓。
（第一幕，第四景，281-89 行）

King Lear　No, I will weep no more. In such a night
　　　　　　To shut me out? Pour on; I will endure
　　　　　　In such a night as this? O Regan, Goneril!
　　　　　　Your old kind father, whose frank heart gave all—
　　　　　　O, that way madness lies; let me shun that;
　　　　　　No more of that. (III, iv, 17-22)

李爾王　　不，我不要再哭了。
　　　　　　在這樣的夜裡
　　　　　　把我關在門外？
　　　　　　大雨儘管下吧
　　　　　　我忍受得了的
　　　　　　在這樣一個夜裡？
　　　　　　啊，麗晶、葛奈麗！
　　　　　　妳們仁慈的老父親
　　　　　　一片赤誠給了妳們所有——
　　　　　　啊！再想下去就要發瘋了
　　　　　　我不要想起那些了；
　　　　　　不再想了。（第三幕，第四景，17-22 行）

Gloucester　The trick of that voice I do well remember;
　　　　　　Is't not the king?
King Lear　Ay, every inch a king! (IV, vi, 106-7)

葛勞賽斯特　這說話的語調我記得很清楚；
　　　　　　這不是國王嗎？
李爾王　　嗯，十足道地的國王！
　　　　　　（第四幕，第六景，106-7 行）

國家圖書館出版品預行編目資料

悅讀莎士比亞故事 .2, 馬克白 & 李爾王 / Charles and
Mary Lamb 著 ; Cosmos Language Workshop 譯 .
一初版 . 一 [臺北市] : 寂天文化，2011.9
　面 ; 公分 .

ISBN　978-986-184-917-1 (25K 平裝附光碟片)

1. 英語　　2. 讀本

805.18　　　　　　　　　　　　　　　100016475

作者	Charles and Mary Lamb
譯者	Cosmos Language Workshop
編輯	陸葵珍
主編	黃鈺云
內文排版	謝青秀
製程管理	林欣穎
出版者	寂天文化事業股份有限公司
電話	02-2365-9739
傳真	02-2365-9835
網址	www.icosmos.com.tw
讀者服務	onlineservice@icosmos.com.tw
出版日期	2011 年 9 月 初版一刷 (250101) 版權所有 請勿翻印
郵撥帳號	1998620-0 寂天文化事業股份有限公司 訂購金額 600(含) 元以上郵資免費 訂購金額 600 元以下者，請外加郵資 60 元 〔 若有破損，請寄回更換，謝謝。〕

CONTENTS

《馬克白》 Practice

I Postreading

1. How do you define ambition? Is there a distinction between a good ambition and a bad one?

2. Do you believe in fortune telling? What do you think is the power, or attraction, of the mysterious unknown? Have you ever consulted on any fortuneteller? Give your experience (if any) and opinions.

2 Vocabulary: Fill in the blanks with the words from the following list.

disclosed	treason	condescension	infirmity	repose
scrupulous	withered	equivocal	afflicted	terms

1. Their _____ skins and wild attire made them look not like any earthly creatures.

2. The king, who out of his royal _____ would oftentimes visit his principal nobility upon gracious _____, came to Macbeth's house.

3. She knew him to be ambitious, but withal to be _____, and not yet prepared for that height of crime which commonly in the end accompanies inordinate ambition.

4. His queen, fearing the dreadful secret would be _____, in great haste dismissed the guests, excusing the _____ of Macbeth as a disorder he was often troubled with.

5. His queen and he had their sleeps _____ with terrible dreams, and the blood of Banquo troubled them not more than the escape of Fleance.

6. Macbeth now began to faint in resolution, and to doubt the _____ speeches of the spirits.

7. He began to envy the condition of Duncan, whom he had murdered, who slept soundly in his grave, against whom _____ had done its worst: steel nor poison, domestic malice nor foreign levies, could hurt him any longer.

8. The queen, who had been the sole partner in Macbeth's wickedness, in whose bosom he could sometimes seek a momentary _____ from those terrible dreams, died.

3 Identification

A. Match the character descriptions with their words and deeds.

Character Descriptions	Words and Deeds

Character Descriptions

1. King of Scotland. He was assassinated by his subject and near kinsman. _____

2. A thane in Scotland whose valour and conduct in the wars was greatly esteemed. _____

3. A bad, ambitious woman, to whom Macbeth communicated the strange prediction of the weird sisters, and its partial accomplishment. _____

4. A thane of Fife, who killed Macbeth in the end. _____

5. The eldest son of the late king, who sought for refuge in the English court after his father was murdered. _____

Words and Deeds

a. "That hope might enkindle you to aim at the throne; but oftentimes these ministers of darkness tell us truths in little things, to betray us into deeds of greatest consequence."

b. "But my heart throbs to know one thing. Tell me, if Banquo's issue shall ever reign in this kingdom?"

c. "Despair thy charm, and let that lying spirit whom thou hast served, tell thee, that I was never born of woman, but was untimely taken from his mother."

d. Who saluted Macbeth with the title of thane of Glamis, the title of thane of Cawdor, and king that shalt be hereafter?

e. Who entered well-pleased with the place where Macbeth's castle was situated, and with the attentions and respect of his honoured hostess, lady Macbeth?

6. A general who never reigned, but his sons after him were kings of Scotland. _____

7. Unearthly figures with women's appearance. They had beards and withered skins. _____

f. Who assigned reason upon reason why Macbeth should not shrink from the bloody business that he had undertaken?

g. Who was the eldest son of the late king, under whom an army was forming in England against Macbeth?

B. Draw a diagram to show the relationships of the characters.

Banquo	Donalbain Duncan	Fleance
Macbeth	Lady Macbeth	Macduff Malcolm

4 Comprehension: Choose the correct answer.

____ 1. Which of the following titles did not the witches salute Macbeth with?
a) Thane of Glamis
b) Thane of Cawdor
c) King of Scotland
d) King of England

____ 2. Which of the following reason did not encourage Macbeth to murder Duncan?
a) Macbeth was ambitious.
b) Macbeth had the swelling hopes that the prediction of the third witch might have its accomplishment.
c) Duncan was a tyrant who had always been cruel to his nobility, in particular to Macbeth.
d) Lady Macbeth spurred on his reluctant purpose and harshly chastised his sluggish resolutions with the valour of her tongue.

____ 3. Why did Lady Macbeth wake to plot the murder of the king herself?
a) Because Macbeth refused to undertake this deed with strong reasons.
b) Because she feared that the natural tenderness of Macbeth's disposition would come between, and defeat the purpose.
c) Because she resented the king who had never love her.
d) Because she was eager to prove that she was more courageous than a man.

____ 4. Which of the following reason cannot explain Macbeth's staggering resolution of murdering the king?
   a) He had not the courage to proceed because the king resembled his father.
   b) He was not only a subject, but also a near kinsman to the king.
   c) He had been the king's host and entertainer that day, whose duty was to shut the door against his murderers.
   d) He stood high in the opinion of all sorts of men, and those honours would surely be stained by the reputation of such a foul murder.

____ 5. Lady Macbeth persuaded her husband to proceed the murder with reasons, which did not include:
   a) She would give him a baby, and milk the babe.
   b) The treasonous deed was.
   c) The action of one short night would give to all their nights and days to come sovereign sway and royalty.
   d) It was practicable to lay the guilt of the treasonous deed upon the drunken sleepy grooms.

____ 6. What did Macbeth do when he heard that Macduff had fled to England, with intent to displace him?
   a) He cried "Glamis hath murdered sleep, and therefore Cawdor shall sleep no more. Macbeth shall sleep no more."
   b) He set upon the castle of Macduff, put his wife and children to the sword, and extended the slaughter to all who claimed the least relationship to Macduff.
   c) He covered his malicious purposes with smiles, and looked innocent, while he was indeed the serpent under the look.
   d) He hanged the messenger alive upon a tree, till famine ended him.

____ 7. Which of the following did not the three spirits bode Macbeth?
   a) To bid him beware of the thane of Fife.
   b) To bid him have no fear, for none of woman born should have power to hurt him.
   c) To comfort him against conspiracies, for he should never be vanquished, until the wood of Birnam to Dunsinane Hill should come against him.

d) To assure him that Banquo's issue shall never reign in Scotland.

___ 8. Who ascended the throne of Duncan the Meek amid the acclamations of the nobles and the people?
a) Macbeth   b) Macduff   c) Malcolm   d) Fleance

5 Discussion

1. What do you think is the main reason that caused this tragedy? Macbeth's ambition? Lady Macbeth's encouragement? The witches' prophecy? Or any other reasons?

2. The story of Macbeth was based on an historical event, on which Shakespeare dramatized into a play. In your opinion, what are the successful elements in this work? The witches and their magic? The suspense and results of the prophecy? The murder scene? The fighting scene? Or the psychological movement of Macbeth?

6 Character Analysis: Consider the mentioned episodes to analyze the characters.

Lady Macbeth

1) her art of covering treacherous purposes with smiles;

2) her denial of Macbeth's milk of human kindness;

3) her undertaking of the murder;

4) her spurring on the reluctant purpose of Macbeth;

5) her desire of sovereign sway and royalty; and

6) her death because of her remorse of guilt and of her inability to bear the public hate.

Macbeth

1) he was enslaved by the witches' prophecy;

2) he shared the prophecy with Lady Macbeth and listened to her words;

3) he struggled between sovereignty and his reputation/responsibility;

4) he murdered Banquo;

5) he was afflicted by terrible dreams;

6) he relied superstitiously on the prophecy;

7) his tyranny and final resolution to fight to death.

7 Challenge

1. The story of Macbeth, written about 400 years ago, was located in Scotland. The cultural and historical backgrounds as well as the language are not easy for modern Taiwanese readers and audiences to understand. Try to adapt the play at your own choice into—

   1. a local version
   2. a shorter version
   3. a modern version

2. You may adapt it in the form you prefer into—

   1. a play
   2. a story
   3. comics
   4. . . .

《馬克白》Answers

2 Vocabulary
A.

1. withered
2. condescension, terms
3. scrupulous
4. disclosed, infirmity
5. afflicted
6. equivocal
7. treason
8. repose

3 Identification
A.

1. e
2. b
3. f
4. c
5. g
6. a
7. d

4 Comprehension

1. d
2. c
3. b
4. a
5. a
6. b
7. d
8. c

《李爾王》 Practice

I Postreading

Do you think that parents or children need to be rewarded according to the quality or the quantity of their love? Give examples (if any) and your arguments.

2 Vocabulary: Explain each of the underlined word in English.

1. The dotage incident to old age had so clouded over his reason that he could not *discern* truth from flattery.

   Discern means _____

2. The king, shocked with this appearance of *ingratitude* in his favourite child, desired her to mend her speech, lest it should mar her fortunes.

   Ingratitude means _____

3. None of the courtiers had the courage to interpose between this *incensed* king and his wrath.

   Incensed means _____

4. King Lear banished this true servant, and *allotted* him but five days to make his preparations for departure.

   Allot means _____

5. Lear could not but perceive this *alteration* in the behaviour of his daughter, but he shut his eyes against it as long as he could.

   Alteration means _____

6. True love and fidelity are no more to be *estranged* by ill, than falsehood and hollow-heartedness can be conciliated by good usage.

   Estrange means _____

7. The hundred knights were all men of choice behaviour and *sobriety* of manners, skilled in all particulars of duty.

Sobriety means _____

8. When, upon *inquiry* for his daughter and her husband, he was told they were weary with travelling all night, and could not see him.

Inquiry means _____

9. But upon examination this spirit proved to be nothing more than one of those poor *lunatics* who are either mad, or feign to be so, the better to extort charity from the *compassionate* country people.

A lunatic means _____ ;

Compassionate means _____

---

3 Identification

A. Match the character's description with the character's words or deeds, and write the character's name.

Character Descriptions

1. King of Britain, who disposed of his kingdom among his daughters in proportions of their affection for him. _____

2. An earl who had been loyal to Lear and was taken into his service by the name of Caius. _____

3. Lear's youngest daughter, who had two suitors-King of France and Duke of Burgundy. _____

4. A jester, who clung to Lear after he had given away his crown, though he could not refrain sometimes from jeering at his master for his

Words and Deeds

a. "But he that has a little tiny wit,/ With heigh ho, the wind and the rain!/ Must make content with his fortunes fit,/ Though the rain it raineth every day."

b. "Creatures that love night, love not such nights as these. This dreadful storm has driven the beasts to their hiding places. Man's nature cannot endure the affliction or the fear."

c. Who ended Cordelia's life in prison after a victorious battle?

d. Who generously granted Cordelia leave to embark for

imprudence in giving all away to his daughters. _____

5. Lear's second daughter, who declared her intention of wedding Edmund when her husband died. _____

6. A natural son of the late earl of Gloucester, who was also the object of Goneril's and Regan's guilty loves. _____

7. Lear's eldest daughter, who made away with her sister by poison, and shortly put an end to her own life. _____

8. Cordelia's husband, who mocked duke of Burgundy's love as running water. _____

England, with a sufficient power to subdue those cruel daughters and their husbands, and restore the old king her father to his throne?

e. Who was wandering about the fields near Dover, in a pitiable condition, stark mad, and singing aloud to himself with a crown upon his head which he had made of straw, and nettles?

f. Who said that Lear was old and foolish, and did not know what he did?

g. Who poisoned her sister out of jealousy?

h. Who said she loved her father according to her duty, neither more nor less?

B. Who are these characters?

| the fool | King of France | Kent | Cordelia |
| Edmund | King Lear | Goneril | Regan |

1. _____ 2. _____ 3. _____ 4. _____

5. _____ 6. _____ 7. _____ 8. _____

4 **Comprehension: Choose the correct answer.**

____ 1. The followings are King Lear's daughters and sons-in-law except _____.
   a) Goneril and the duke of Albany.
   b) Regan and the duke of Cornwall.
   c) Cordelia and the duke of Burgundy.
   d) Cordelia and the king of France.

____ 2. How did King Lear intend to part his kingdom among his daughters?
   a) In proportions as their affection for him.
   b) In order of their ages.
   c) In degrees of how he favoured them.
   d) By consulting his courtiers.

____ 3. What did King Lear retain for himself after he preposterously disposed of his kingdom?
   a) The crown.
   b) The revenue.
   c) The execution of government.
   d) The name of king and a hundred knights.

____ 4. Why did Goneril tell Lear that his staying in her palace was inconvenient?
   a) Because Caius always tripped up her steward's heels.
   b) Because she esteemed his old age a useless burden, and his attendants an unnecessary expense.
   c) Because Lear kept the knights who only served to fill her court with riot and feasting.
   d) Because she could no longer take proper care of him due to her illness.

____ 5. What did Lear do in a stormy and rainy night when his daughters persisted in their resolution not to admit his followers?
   a) He stayed under the same roof with these ungrateful daughters.
   b) He went down on his knees, and begged of his daughters for food and raiment.
   c) He encountered the utmost fury of the storm abroad and sallied forth to combat with the elements.
   d) He cursed that neither of them might never have a child, or if they had, that it might live to return that scorn and contempt upon them which they had shown to him.

____ 6. The good Caius plainly perceived that Lear was not in his perfect mind, but that his daughters' ill usage had really made him _____.
   a) Show much of spleen and rashness.
   b) Go mad.
   c) Guided little by reason and much by passion.
   d) Terrified by spirits.

___7. Which of the following was not the reason that caused Lear's madness?
   a) His two wicked daughters by little and little have abated him of all his train and all respect.
   b) He had been through a hard change-from a king to a beggar, and from commanding millions to be without one attendant.
   c) He was old and wanted discretion.
   d) He was vexed at having so foolishly given away his kingdom.

___ 8. Who promised the skillful physicians all her gold and jewels for the recovery of the old king from the madness?
   a) Cordelia.   b) Lear himself.   c) Kent.   d) the fool.

5 Discussion

1. What do you think of old age? Do you think that Lear made the mistakes because he was "old and foolish" as he claimed himself to be? Why or why not?

2. Was the fool really a "fool" as his appellation suggested? How do you see him and Lear as two roles? Would it stand to reason that there is a contrast of foolishness and wisdom between them?

6 Character Study

A tragic flaw refers to a protagonist's certain weakness or feature, which gradually leads the character or the play to a tragedy. Do you consider that King Lear has a tragic flaw? Why or why not?

7 Challenge

Imagine yourself as a courtier in Lear's court. You know Lear and her daughters well. Explain and comment on their deeds, their backgrounds while growing up, their interactions, their characteristics, and if possible, some episodes from the past that could foreshadow this tragedy.

3 Identification

A.

1. e
2. b
3. h
4. a
5. f
6. c
7. g
8. d

B.

1. King Lear
2. Kent
3. Cordelia
4. the fool
5. Regan
6. Edmund
7. Goneril
8. King of France

4 Comprehension

1. c
2. a
3. d
4. b
5. c
6. b
7. c
8. a

P.26 在「仁厚鄧肯」國王統治蘇格蘭時,有一個叫做馬克白的顯赫貴族勛爵。馬克白是國王的近親,因為沙場上表現英勇,指揮作戰有功,在朝廷備受敬重。最近,他才殲滅一支為數眾多並有挪威軍隊相助的叛軍。

贏得這場激戰後,馬克白和班科這兩名蘇格蘭大將凱旋而歸。途中,他們經過一片枯乾的荒原時,被三個長相怪異的人擋住去路。她們看似女人,卻長著鬍鬚,皮膚乾皺,打扮古怪,簡直不像人類。馬克白先開口和她們打招呼,她們卻狀似生氣,個個都把皺巴巴的手指壓在乾癟的嘴唇上,示意他安靜。之後,她們其中一人稱馬克白為「葛雷密斯爵士」,向他致敬。

P.28 馬克白將軍很訝異這些人居然認識他,更令他驚訝的是,第二個接著致敬的人稱他為「考德領主」。這榮衛他可擔待不起啊,而第三個人更竟是對他說:「萬歲!未來的國王!」這種像是預言的打招呼方式,讓馬克白驚愕不已。畢竟,只要國王的兒子在世,他就不可能登基為王。

P.29 接著,她們三人轉過身向著班科,打啞謎似地對他說:「位階不如馬克白,卻更勝一籌!不如馬克白幸運,卻又更有福!」她們預言他雖然不會稱王,但他的後代將會成為蘇格蘭王。說罷,三人就化做一陣輕煙消失。看到這番景象,兩名將軍這才明白她們是三女神或巫婆之類的人。

他們愣在原地,納悶方才碰到的怪事。此時,國王的信差抵達。信差傳送聖旨,冊封馬克白為考德領主。

P.30 馬克白著實震驚,事實竟神奇地吻合了女巫的預言,他整個人呆住,答不出話來。此時此刻,對於第三個女巫的預言,他的願望愈來愈強——希望預言也會如法實現,讓他終有一天成為蘇格蘭王。

馬克白轉身向班科說:「女巫對我的預言神奇地應驗了,你難道不希望你的子孫也會稱王嗎?」

P.31 將軍答道:「這種願望只會讓人貪圖王位。像女巫這種邪惡的使者,常會跟我們透露一點事實,然後讓我們一失足成千古恨。」

無奈女巫們的缺德暗示,深深烙印在馬克白的腦海裡,他根本無心理會好心班科的忠告，此後整個心思都懸念著要如何篡奪蘇格蘭王位。

馬克白對妻子講述了三女巫的奇怪預言和部分預言的應驗。馬克白夫人是個野心勃勃的壞女人，為了丈夫和自己的榮顯，可以不擇手段。

P.32 馬克白委決不下，一想到要殺人，他就良心不安。但馬克白夫人極力慫恿他，不斷強調要實現美好預言，就非殺掉國王不可。

國王時常屈駕拜訪大貴族。這時，他正好在兒子梅爾康和杜納班的陪同下，來到馬克白的住處。為了榮耀馬克白的輝煌戰績，國王還帶了眾多爵士和隨從。

P.33 馬克白的城堡位置座落極佳，空氣芬芳清新，所以城堡各處的飛簷扶壁，只要是適於築巢之處，就會有燕巢。只要是燕子繁殖出沒的地方，空氣總是特別清新。

國王一走進城堡，就感到神清氣爽。女主人馬克白夫人對他的殷勤和尊敬，也同樣令他心花怒放。誰知，夫人善詭計，笑藏刀，無瑕花下藏毒蛇。

P.34 這晚，旅途勞頓的國王早早上了床，照例由兩名寢宮侍從伴睡兩側。國王對這次的招待分外心滿意足，就寢前特地賞賜禮物給大臣們。他還送了一枚貴重的鑽戒給馬克白夫人，並稱她是「最親切的女主人」。

子夜時分，大地一片死寂，惡夢打擾睡眠中的人們，外頭只有狼和謀殺者在遊蕩。馬克白夫人此時醒來，打算謀殺國王。

她一名女子實不需沾惹如此駭人之事，但怕只怕軟心腸的丈夫下不了手。她知道他是有野心，可是生性謹慎，除非企圖心夠強，要不然他是不會準備動手殺人的。

P.36 她已經勸服他把國王殺掉，但擔心他決心不夠，怕他那比她還要仁慈的柔順個性礙事，壞了這事。

所以，倒不如她自己動手吧。她拿著匕首，走向國王的床。國王的兩個寢侍早就被她給灌醉，正睡得不省人事，怠忽職守，而旅途的疲累也讓鄧肯睡得香甜。她仔細端詳國王，覺得他沈睡的臉龐和父親有些相像。這麼一想之後，竟沒勇氣行凶了。

P.37 她回去和丈夫商量，丈夫卻愈見躊躇，心下琢磨各種不該行兇的理由。首先，他不只是臣子，也是國王的親戚。再者，他今天做東道主，按主客禮法，他本應加強守備，防範刺殺，更甭說是要自己去拿刀行刺了。

他又想，鄧肯國王公正仁慈，愛民惜臣，而且還特別抬舉他呢。上天會特別眷顧這種國王的，要是國王慘遭不測，子民必會誓言報仇。此外，他受到國王的寵愛，眾人對他的風評因此特別好，他怎能讓謀殺這種醜名來玷污原有的榮譽呢？

P. 38 馬克白夫人看出丈夫內心掙扎，善念愈來愈多，有意放棄謀殺計畫。然而，她，一個女人，可不是這麼容易就會讓壞念頭搖動的。她開始在他耳邊啐啐不休，對他進行洗腦，提出他不應該就此退縮的千百種理由，並強調殺人之事何等容易，一眨眼就會結束，短短一夜的一個行動，會讓他們後半輩子享有至高無上的權勢。

她又恥笑他打退堂鼓，數落他意志不堅，膽小怕事。她表示，她是哺乳過嬰兒的，疼惜在自己懷中吮奶的嬰兒，她知道那滋味有多美妙。可是，只要她發過誓要殺嬰兒，就像他發過誓要殺國王那樣，那麼就算嬰兒當時正對著她微笑，她也會二話不說就把嬰兒從她懷裡扔出去，摔得它腦漿迸裂。

P. 40 她繼續說，只要把事情誣賴到那兩個醉得昏睡的寢侍頭上，兩三下就可以搞定。她鼓舌搖唇地斥責他意志薄弱，結果他幹血腥勾當的膽量就又被激發了。

馬克白手握匕首，悄悄摸黑走向鄧肯睡覺的房間。走著走著，他好像看到空中有另一把匕首，匕首的刀柄朝著他，刀刃和刀尖都淌著血滴。當他伸手要抓住那把刀時，卻撲了個空，這才知道那不過是幻覺，因為他腦子裡亂哄哄的，滿是謀殺念頭。

P. 41 他擺脫掉恐懼感，走進國王房間，一刀讓國王斃命。就在此時，一個寢侍在夢裡大笑，另一個則在夢裡大叫：「殺人啊！」這一叫，把兩人都驚醒。兩人於是唸誦一小段禱文，最後，其中一人唸：「上帝保佑我們！」另一人唸：「阿們！」然後就囑咐自己繼續睡覺。

當那人唸完「上帝保佑我們」時，在一旁聽他們禱告的馬克白，努力要跟著唸「阿們」，誰知那兩個字卻卡在喉嚨裡，怎麼也吐不出來。

P. 43 後來他又好像聽到有人喊著：「別再睡了！馬克白殺死睡眠了，殺死了清白無辜、滋養生命的睡眠了！」聲音繼續迴盪整座房子：「別再睡了！葛拉米殺死睡眠了，所以考德無法成眠了，馬克白再也無法成眠了。」

馬克白滿腦子都是可怕的想像，他走回專心聆聽他動靜的妻子跟前，妻子還以為他刺殺不成壞了事呢。她看他心神恍惚地走進來，逕自責怪他太軟弱，要他去洗掉手上的血漬，她自己則拿著匕首，把血塗在侍從的臉上，以便嫁禍給他們。

P.44 紙包不住火，凶殺案隔天清晨就曝光。儘管馬克白和夫人強裝悲痛，寢侍謀殺國王的證據也很充分（匕首是從他們身上搜出來的，而且兩人臉上又沾有血跡），不過大家還是認為馬克白的嫌疑最大。畢竟，比起兩個可憐糊塗的寢侍，馬克白謀殺國王才大大有利可圖呢。鄧肯的兩個兒子雙雙逃逸，長子梅爾康逃往英格蘭宮廷請求庇護，么子杜納班則逃往愛爾蘭。

王位本來應該由國王的兒子來繼承，但經他們這麼一放棄，就輪到馬克白加冕為王了。至此，三女巫的預言完全實現。

P.46 登上王位後，馬克白和皇后仍心懸著三女巫的其他預言：馬克白雖已稱王，但後繼的王不是他的子嗣，卻是班科的子孫。一想到這裡，再想到自己雙手血腥、犯了可怕的罪，卻拱手把王位讓給班科的後代，實在是很不甘心。三女巫對他的預言一一神奇地應驗，為了讓其他預言無法實現，他們決定把班科和他的兒子也一併解決掉。

為此他們舉辦一場鴻門宴，盛大邀請所有大領主，尤其特別隆重邀請班科和他兒子弗林斯。

P.47 當晚，馬克白在他們父子前往王宮的途中埋伏刺客，班科當場被殺，弗林斯則在混戰中脫逃。

此後，蘇格蘭王就從弗林斯開始嫡傳，一直傳到蘇格蘭的詹姆士六世兼英格蘭的詹姆士一世，並由其統一了英格蘭和蘇格蘭。

P.48 在這場晚宴上，皇后的態度極盡親切雍容。這位女主人表現得舉止得體，彬彬有禮，在場的人莫不對她產生好感。馬克白和領主貴族們侃侃而談，他表示，要是他的好友班科也在場，那他就集國內眾傑於一堂了。又說他寧可班科因為忘了出席而責備他，也不願他遭遇不測而哀悼他。

就在他這說話的當兒，被謀殺的班科的鬼魂走了進來，搶先坐上馬克白原本要就座的位子。儘管馬克白膽子大，不畏魔鬼，但這恐怖的景象，還是嚇得他面如土色。他怯懦地楞在那裡，目不轉睛盯著班科的鬼魂。

P.49 皇后和貴族們什麼也沒看到，只見他直視著空椅子（他們這麼想），便以為他一時精神錯亂。皇后斥責他，小聲跟他說那不過是幻覺，就像他謀殺鄧肯時看到空中出現匕首一樣。但鬼魂並沒有消失，馬克白顧不了旁人，逕自與鬼魂說起話來。他語無倫次，語帶玄機，皇后怕他會把可怕的秘密給抖出來，就藉口說馬克白的老毛病又犯了，連忙送客。

P.51 馬克白被這些恐怖的幻象所苦。他和皇后惡夢連連，殺了班科讓他們不安，弗林斯的脫逃讓他們憂心忡忡。弗林斯是日後眾國王的先祖，會讓他們自己的後代無法登基為王。他們因此擔心受怕，心懸不下。馬克白於是決定去找三女巫，一探結果究竟如何。

他在荒原的山洞裡找到了三女巫。她們早預知他會來，所以正著手可怖的符咒，好招喚地獄的鬼魂來向她們透露未來。

P.52 她們使用嚇人材料，包括蟾蜍、蝙蝠、蛇、蠑螈眼、狗舌頭、蜥蜴腿、貓頭鷹翅、龍麟、狼牙、鹹海鯊魚的胃、木乃伊女巫、有毒人參的根部（要在黑夜時去挖才有效）、山羊膽、猶太人的肝臟、在基地裡生根的紫杉插枝，以及死去小孩的手指等等。

先把這些材料扔進大鍋或鍋爐裡熬煮，完全滾沸時再倒進狒狒的血，加以冷卻。接著加入吃掉親生幼豬的母豬的血，再把殺人犯留在絞架上的油垢丟進火堆裡。施了這些咒法，地獄的鬼魂就不得不回答她們的問題了。

P.53 三女巫問馬克白，看他是要問她們，還是要問她們的鬼魂主人。剛剛親眼所瞧的可怕儀式並沒有嚇到馬克白，他面無懼色地說：「鬼魂在哪裡？我要見他們。」她們就把鬼魂喚來，一共來了三個。

第一個升起來的鬼魂頭戴盔甲，他直呼馬克白的名字，囑咐他要留意費輔領主。馬克白道過謝，他也早就對費輔的領主麥德夫有所猜忌了。

第二個來的鬼魂是個全身血淋淋的小孩子。他同樣直呼馬克白的名字，要他不用害怕，大可對凡人的力量嗤之以鼻，因為打娘胎出來的人是傷不了他的，還勸他心狠手辣，盡可肆無忌憚。

「那你姑且活著吧，麥德夫！」馬克白喊道：「我幹嘛怕你呢？可惜我還是得把事情做到萬無一失──你休想活命！恐懼不過子虛烏有，就算天打雷劈，我也照樣倒頭大睡。」

P.55 第二個鬼魂退下之後，第三個來的鬼魂也是個小孩，他手擎一株樹，頭戴王冠。他叫著馬克白的名字，要他寬心，不用擔心有人謀反，除非勃南樹林移到丹新南丘來向他進攻，否則他決不會戰敗。

19

「好預兆！好啊！」馬克白叫道：「誰有能耐把森林連根拔起、移動易位呢？看來我不會死於非命，可以安享天年了。不過還有一件事我很想知道，要是你知道就告訴我吧，到底這個王國會不會被班科的後代所統治？」

P.57 話才説完，鍋爐沒入地下，響起嘈雜聲樂，有八個國王似的幽靈從馬克白面前走過，其中走在最後面的正是班科。班科手持一面鏡子，鏡中映出許多人影。他渾身血淋淋，指著鏡中人影，對著馬克白微笑。馬克白知道那些人影就是班科的後代，將繼馬克白之後統治蘇格蘭。接著一陣輕柔音樂，女巫們婆娑起舞，表示職責已盡，向馬克白示意後旋即消失。從此刻開始，馬克白心頭盡盤旋著各種血腥恐怖的念頭。

　　一走出女巫的洞穴後，馬克白就得到費輔的領主麥德夫逃往英格蘭的消息。麥德夫加入由先王的長子梅爾康所率領的反抗軍，打算推翻馬克白，擁護正統王儲梅爾康登基為王。

P.58 馬克白聽了勃然大怒，立刻攻打麥德夫的城堡，把領主留在城裡的妻兒都殺掉，連同所有曾跟隨麥德夫的人也一併誅殺殆盡。

P.59 馬克白的這些行為，使大貴族們人心叛離。他們能逃則逃，加入梅爾康和麥德夫在英格蘭組成的強大軍隊，而軍隊正往蘇格蘭步步逼近。其餘因畏於馬克白而不敢有所行動的人，也都暗地裡希望梅爾康的軍隊得勝。馬克白的新兵招募，進行得很緩慢。

　　暴君令人痛恨，馬克白得不到愛戴，眾人猜忌他，這下倒讓他開始羨慕起被他害死的鄧肯了。雖然鄧肯遭到最惡毒的暗算，但起碼能在墓裡好好安睡，什麼刀槍毒藥或是內憂外患，都再也傷不了他了。

P.60 就在這喧騰之際，馬克白這起罪行的唯一共犯——皇后，竟撒手歸陰了。兩人夜裡被惡夢所纏時，他偶爾還可以在皇后懷裡得到一時的喘息。如今大概因為良心不安，民怨眾恨，她承受不了終而自盡，留下馬克白孑然無依，不再有人愛他、關心他，沒人可以商討腹中的陰謀詭計。

P.61 馬克白漸漸變得厭世，想一死了之。但逐漸逼近的梅爾康軍隊，又激起他曾經有過的勇氣，他決定如自己所説的「身披盔甲」地戰死。另外，女巫們的空口白話也讓他有過了頭的自信。他記得鬼魂説，打娘胎出生的人都傷不了他，他永遠都不會吃敗仗，除非把勃南樹林移到丹新南，而他認為那根本是天方夜譚。

P.62 他把自己關在城堡裡。城堡固若金湯，攻克不易。他面色凝重，等著梅爾康的到來。一天，一個被嚇得臉色蒼白的傳令兵跑來，幾乎無法開口上奏所見之事。他一口咬定説，他在山上站哨時往勃南看去，發現樹林在移動。

「你這撒謊的奴才！」馬克白大叫：「如果你膽敢謊報，我就把你吊在旁邊那棵樹上，讓你活活餓死。如果你説的是真的，你大可以也這樣吊死我。」馬克白的信念開始動搖，他懷疑鬼魂所言話中藏話。只要勃南樹林不會移到丹新南，他就無所擔憂，但現在樹林真的移動了！

P.63 他説：「假使傳令兵所説不假，我們還是武裝出城吧。我們逃不了，但也不能坐以待斃，反正我開始厭倦陽光了，希望生命早點有個了結。」説完這些絕望的話，他朝著正攻向城堡的軍隊衝過去。

傳令兵以為樹林在移動，這種奇異景象不難解釋。圍攻的軍隊穿越勃南樹林時，具有謀略之將領的梅爾康，指示每位士兵都砍下一根樹枝，把樹枝捧在面前，以掩蓋軍隊的實際人數。遠遠看過去，拿著樹枝前進的軍隊就把傳令兵給嚇壞了。

鬼魂的話其實也應驗了，只是和馬克白所理解的不同，這讓他泰半的信心頓時消失。

P.64 一時短兵相接，交戰激烈。自稱與馬克白同盟的人僅給予他片面支援，因為他們實際上痛恨這個暴君，心向著梅爾康及麥德夫。不過，馬克白還是異常兇猛，把敵人打得落花流水，直到與麥德夫正面相逢。

看到麥德夫，他想起鬼魂的警告他説，眾人之中他最要小心躲避的就是麥德夫。他本想躲開，可是麥德夫尋遍整個戰場就是要找他，不讓他離開，一場激戰即將展開。麥德夫痛罵馬克白殺害他的妻兒，馬克白因滿門的血債良心不安，遲遲不肯動手開戰。麥德夫繼續挑釁，斥責他是暴君、兇手、地獄狗、惡棍。

P.65 這時，馬克白想到鬼魂説打娘胎出生的人傷不了他，於是自信滿滿地笑著對麥德夫説：「麥德夫，你只是在白費力氣。你要是傷得了我，那你大概也能用劍在空中劃出條線了。我有法術保護，凡是打娘胎出生的人都傷不了我。」

P.66 「你的符咒失效了！」麥德夫説：「讓你信奉的那些騙人鬼來告訴你吧，麥德夫不是打娘胎出生的，他不像一般人那樣出生下來，他是提早就從母親的肚子裡被取出來的。」

「詛咒告訴我那話的舌頭吧！」馬克白渾身顫慄地說道，他感到他最後的把握也喪失了。「但願人們永遠不再聽信巫婆和騙人鬼的那些曖昧謊言，他們話中藏話來欺騙我們，表面上看起來應驗，卻用不一樣的理解方式來讓我們希望落空。我不會和你戰鬥的。」

P. 67 「那我就饒了你！」麥德夫輕蔑地說：「我們要把你公開展示，就像展示怪物一樣，掛張告示牌，上面寫著：『暴君在此，供人觀賞。』」

「休想！」馬克白在絕望中重現勇氣，他說：「只要我活著，就不會在梅爾康那小子跟前屈膝低頭，讓賤民詛咒辱罵我。即使勃南樹林移到了丹新南，即使你這個不是打娘胎出生的人要跟我作對，我還是要放手搏鬥到底。」

說完這番發狂似的話，他縱身撲向麥德夫。麥德夫經過一番奮戰，終於戰勝馬克白，並把他的頭顱砍下，作為獻禮送給正統的年輕王儲梅爾康。梅爾康從陰謀篡位的人手中取回睽違已久的政權，在貴族與人民的歡呼聲中，登上「仁厚鄧肯」的王位。

《李爾王》中譯

P. 84 不列顛國王李爾有三個女兒：嫁給歐伯尼公爵的葛奈麗、嫁給康沃公爵的麗晶，以及待字閨中的小蔻蒂莉。正待在李爾的王宮裡的法王和伯根第公爵，都為向蔻蒂莉求婚特地前來。

老國王年事已高，加以政務繁忙，讓他甚感疲憊。他年逾八十了，決定不再過問政事，打算把國家交給年輕的一代去管理，好讓自己可以好好走完風燭殘年，準備棄世。

P. 85 於是他把三個女兒喚到跟前，想親耳聽聽哪一個女兒最愛他，而他也可以依此來決定如何分配王國。

長女葛奈麗說，她對父親的愛是言語所無法表達的，父親比她自己的眼睛、性命或自由都還珍貴。對於李爾這個問題，用幾句真心的好話來回答就夠了，不過卻正因虛情假意，反倒信口就編出了一堆花言巧語。

聽到女兒確言切切的愛，國王龍心大悅，不疑有他。父愛油然而生，他就把廣大王國的三分之一，賜給了大女兒和大女婿。

P. 86 國王接著喚二女兒，問了她同樣的問題。麗晶不只和大姐是一丘之貉，口才更是不輸大姐。她說大姐的話都還不足以表達她對父王的愛，因為沈浸在親愛父王的父愛裡頭，其他的一切快樂都霎時變得索然無味。

看到孩子這麼愛自己，李爾覺得自己真是有福氣啊。聽完麗晶動人的話，他也同樣把王國的三分之一封給麗晶和她丈夫，和葛奈麗同得其份。

最後他轉向小女兒蔻蒂莉。蔻蒂莉一向是最讓他窩心的了，他問完蔻蒂莉，暗忖她必定會說出跟姐姐一樣動聽的話來讓他高興，甚至有過之而無不及，因為他向來最寵愛她。

P. 88 蔻蒂莉知道姐姐們根本言不由衷，她們只不過是想哄騙國王交出領土，好在國王有生之年時就可以接管王國。蔻蒂莉因此對她們的阿諛奉承反感至極。結果，小女兒最後只回答說——她愛國王陛下，乃出於本分，恰如其分。

聽到自己最鍾愛的女兒說出這番不領情似的話，國王大為震驚，要她重新考慮自己的用詞，修正說法，以免自毀前程。

蔻蒂莉回答，他是育她愛她的父親，她跪乳孝思，必會服從他、敬愛他、景仰他。可惜她無法像姐姐那樣誇大其詞，或是保證父親是她世上惟一所愛的人。

P.90 如果姐姐們真的只愛父親一人，那怎麼又會有個丈夫呢？要是她結婚了，她相信另一半也想擁有她一半的感情、關懷和責任。如果她只愛父親一人，那就不可能像姐姐那樣去嫁人了。

但事實上，蔻蒂莉才真如姐姐們所佯言地那樣深愛著年邁的父親。在平時，她會用為人女兒的態度，說些更親熱的話，直接明白地向父親表示敬愛。然而，看到姐姐們藉著虛偽的奉承，得到豐厚的賞賜，她就保留了自己的態度，說出了不是很中聽的話——因為她想她所能做的最好事情，就是默默地愛著父親，以表明自己的感情沒有摻雜利害關係，對父親的愛也不求回報。她的告白雖不動聽，卻遠比姐姐們的話真切誠懇呀。

P.92 然而，李爾卻認為她那種平實的回答很傲慢，因而大動肝火。李爾在年輕輝煌的時候就很魯莽暴躁，現在加上人老了，腦子不管用，碰到這種事，根本也看不清是真實還是奉承，是虛偽話還是真心話了。他一怒之下，把原本打算留給蔻蒂莉的三分之一王國收回，平分給兩個姐姐和姐夫歐柏尼與康沃公爵。李爾喚他們過來，在眾臣面前將冠冕賜予他們，把所有的權力、稅收和國政一併交給他們。他自己放棄了國王的一切職權，僅保留國王頭銜和一百名騎士以做為隨從，打算按月輪流居住在兩個女兒的宮殿裡。

P.93 看到李爾行事這樣衝動，王國分配得這麼荒唐，群臣無不錯愕惋惜。然而，除了肯特伯爵，大家都不敢出聲，深怕冒犯了正在氣頭上的國王。肯特伯爵想替蔻蒂莉說說話，但才一出口，激動的李爾便以處死做為要脅，要他住口，但好心的肯特並沒有因此退卻。

P.94 肯特向來對李爾忠心耿耿，敬他如君，愛他如父，從他如主。肯特視自己的生命價值在於擊退李爾的敵人，為了保衛李爾的安全，他視死如歸。現在，即使李爾的敵人就是李爾自己，這個忠僕也沒忘記自己的原則，仍要為了李爾好而勇敢地反對李爾。要是他現在無禮了，那也是因為李爾變得很沒有理智。

P.95 他一向是國王最可靠的幕僚，一如以往在做許多重大決策一樣，他現在請求李爾接受他的諫言，採納他的忠告。他勸國王三思，收回草率的成命。他敢用性命做擔保，擔保小女兒的孝心決不亞於姐姐，而她的回答之所以冷漠低調，正是因為她沒有半點虛情假意。

要是在位者為諂言所迷，良臣就得直言無諱。肯特的性命都任隨李爾處置了，李爾的恫嚇，又怎能嚇阻得了他呢？這些都無法阻礙他忠言直諫的本分。

然而，好心伯爵肯特的誠實坦白只是更加激怒了國王。國王成了發瘋似的病人，要殺掉自己的醫生，好捍衛足以致命的疾病。國王下令流放這個忠僕，限他五天之內離開，如果在第六天時，還讓他看到他在不列顛，那他就必死無疑。

P. 96 於是肯特向國王告別，表示自己也知道選擇這種直諫方式的結果就是被流放。在他離開之前，他還祝福正直慎言的蔻蒂莉能夠得到神的庇護，並但願她的姐姐們能夠將動聽的話付諸實現。他離去時，又說他在異鄉還是會不改變自己這樣的做法。

李爾召見法王和伯根第公爵，說明他對小女兒所做的決定。現在她不再得父親的歡心，分不到半點財產，只能自求多福，他想知道他們是否還想娶蔻蒂莉。

P. 97 伯根第公爵聽了之後便婉拒這場婚事，他可不想娶這樣的蔻蒂莉為妻。至於法王，他明白蔻蒂莉失去父王寵愛的癥結在於她直言骨鯁，不若姐姐那般舌燦蓮花。於是他牽起這位年輕女孩的手，說她的美德是一份勝於國土的嫁妝。他請蔻蒂莉告別姐姐，告別待她刻薄的父親跟他走，做他的皇后，在氣候宜人的法國做女王，擁有比姐姐們更錦繡的領土。

P. 98 最後，他用輕蔑的口吻稱伯根第公爵是「流水公爵」，因為他對這位年輕女孩的愛，一眨眼就像流水一樣全流光了。

蔻蒂莉淌著淚水向姐姐道別，並請她們如所宣稱那樣地愛護父親。姐姐們聽了很火大，說她們知道自己的本分，不用她多嘴。兩人還謔笑地說，她只管好好伺候她丈夫就行了，因為她丈夫已經把她視為命運送給他的施捨了。

最後蔻蒂莉帶著沉重的心情離去，她知道姐姐們為人狡猾，她是多麼希望可以由比較可靠的人來照料父親呀。

P. 99 蔻蒂莉一走，兩個姐姐就開始露出了邪惡的真面目。李爾依約住在大女兒葛奈麗那裡還不到一個月，就發現女兒言行不一。

這卑鄙女兒得到父王所能贈予的一切還不夠，還想把父王頭上的皇冠給摘下來。父親保留的皇家頭銜、僅餘的國王乾癮，都讓她心頭生怨。

P. 100 她一看到父王或他的百名騎士就一肚子氣。要是撞見父王，她就板起面孔。如果老人家要跟她說話，她就裝病或找理由迴避他。很顯然地，她分明就把這個老頭當成累贅，認為給他隨從根本是不必要的開銷。僕人有樣學樣，女兒對國王的怠慢和（恐怕）女兒暗地裡的唆使，讓僕人也跟著故意冷落國王。他們不是不聽從他的命令，就是傲慢地佯裝沒聽到。

P. 101 李爾不可能沒感受到女兒態度上的轉變，但他盡量假裝沒事，因為人們總是不願意承認痛苦是自己的錯誤和頑固所造成的。

對方要是真誠忠信，就算待他刻薄，他也不會離開；對方要是虛偽裝假，就算對他再好，他也不會感激你的。這種說法用在好心伯爵肯特的身上，是最適切不過了。肯特被李爾流放，萬一被發現他人還在不列顛，那就只有死路一條。然而，只要還有機會為主子效命，他就甘願冒著被處死的危險而留下來。

P. 102 看哪！可憐的忠僕有時不得不將就屈辱，把自己假扮成身分低賤的樣子來偽裝自己。不過這並不卑賤可恥，因為他是為了恪盡職責！

好心伯爵放下所有身段，撇下豪華生活，喬裝成傭人，請求服侍國王。國王不察此人就是肯特，只知聽他率直甚至粗拙的應話，還讓他覺得舒坦呢。（因為這跟那些油腔滑舌的諂言不一樣，看到女兒的口是心非，李爾早厭倦了花言巧語。）他們兩人很快談妥，李爾答應收肯特為私傭。肯特自稱為凱爾斯，李爾怎麼也沒料到，他就是自己曾經最鍾愛且意氣風發的肯特伯爵。

P. 103 不多久，凱爾斯就抓到機會表現他對主子的忠誠與敬愛：就在當天，葛奈麗的管家對李爾傲慢無禮。管家無疑暗中受到了女主人的教唆，不但給李爾臉色看，又口出蔑言。凱爾斯不能忍受他這樣公然地羞辱國王陛下，二話不說立刻伸出腳將他絆倒，然後把這個不知禮數的僕人扔進狗屋裡。凱爾斯這種貼心的舉動，讓李爾和他愈來愈親近。

P. 104 李爾的朋友並不只有肯特。在李爾還擁有宮殿時，他的宮廷裡有一個愚者（或稱弄臣）。在那個時代，國王和權貴有豢養「愚者」（一般都是這樣叫他們的）的風氣，好讓自己在繁重的公務之外，得以解悶。儘管愚者身位低微，卻非常忠誠。李爾放棄王位之後，他那位卑微的愚者仍隨侍著他，用些詼諧的話來逗他開心。不過，愚者偶爾也忍不住揶揄他的主子，笑他草草率率就退位，把一切都過繼給女兒。他作打油詩來說這些女兒們：

P. 105 （她們）因為驚喜掉眼淚，
他為悲傷開口唱，
堂堂國君捉迷藏，
愚者之間穿梭跑。

愚者多的是這種不羈的詩詞歌曲，即使在葛奈麗面前，這位逗趣老實的愚者照樣大吐肺腑之言。他犀利地挖苦譏諷她，譬如把國王比喻為籬雀，說小布穀鳥哺乳長大後，就會把籬雀的腦袋瓜給咬下來，以報答養育之恩。又說，要是馬匹由馬車來牽著走，笨驢也會看得出來（意思是說，女兒本該聽從父親的，現在卻權凌父親）。他還說，李爾不再是李爾了，不過是徒具李爾的軀殼。愚者這樣肆無忌憚的發言，曾挨過一兩次小心吃鞭子的警告。

P. 106 李爾開始感受到這些冷落和不敬，但不肖女兒要他這糊塗父親嚐到的滋味還不只這些。

她現在跟他挑明講，只要他堅持保留百名騎士的編制，那他就不便留在她的宮殿裡。她說這種編制既無意義又花錢，數落騎士只會在她的宮廷裡大吵大鬧、吃吃喝喝。她要求他裁減騎士的數量，留下和他年紀相仿的老人在身邊就可以了。

李爾聽她這麼一講，以為是自己耳背眼花了。他真不敢相信說出這番刻薄話的人，竟是自己的女兒呀。他不敢相信他給了她皇冠，她卻要裁減他的侍從，不願給他應享的晚年。

女兒堅持這個不肖的要求，氣炸了的李爾直呼她是「可恨的鳶」，盡會瞎扯胡扯。的確，那一百名騎士都是品行優良、正經持重的一時之選，謹守一切本分，並不如女兒所說的那樣吃喝喧鬧。

P. 108 他命人備妥馬匹，帶著他的百名騎士前往二女兒麗晶的住處。他嘴裡唸著數典忘祖這件事，形容那簡直就是鐵石心腸的妖魔，一個孩子要是不知飲水思源，就會比海妖還可怕。

他用嚇人的字眼詛咒大女兒葛奈麗，咒她絕子絕孫，就算她有了小孩，小孩也會用同樣鄙視輕蔑的態度來回報她，好讓她知道有個忘恩負義的孩子，是如何比被毒蛇咬到還痛苦。

葛奈麗的丈夫歐伯尼公爵擔心李爾會認為這種不義之事他也有份，便想向李爾解釋，但李爾不聽他說完，只顧忿忿地叫人備好馬鞍，帶著隨從往二女兒麗晶的住處出發。

P. 109 李爾現在想想，和她姐姐比起來，蔻蒂莉的過錯（如果也算是過錯的話）是多麼微不足道呀。想著想著，他不禁流下老淚，接著又覺得很羞愧，因為自己竟讓葛奈麗這樣的畜生給欺負得流下男兒淚。

麗晶和丈夫向來把他們的皇宮弄得富麗奢華。李爾先派遣臣僕凱爾斯捎信給二女兒，以便準備迎接他和眾隨從。

P. 110 不過，看來葛奈麗似乎搶先一步寄信給麗晶。她在信上說父親剛愎自用，性情乖張，並勸她不要收留他隨身的那一大群侍從。

葛奈麗的信差和凱爾斯同時抵達，兩人碰了頭。那信差原來就是凱爾斯的那位死對頭管家，凱爾斯曾因他對李爾無禮而把他絆倒。

　　凱爾斯不喜歡這傢伙的調調，又懷疑他此行不懷好意，開口便斥罵他，要跟他決鬥。那傢伙拒絕決鬥，凱爾斯一陣義憤，痛扁了他一頓，誰教他愛挑撥離間，送來這缺德的信呢？麗晶和丈夫得知這件事之後，也不管他是父王派來的信差，理應受到最高禮遇，就命人把凱爾斯銬上腳鐐。

P. 111 是以國王進入城堡時，首先迎接他的就是坐相狼狽的忠僕凱爾斯。

　　但這不過是二女兒迎接李爾的一個預告罷了，還有更惡劣的事呢！李爾說要見女兒和女婿，僕人卻回說他們趕了一整晚的路，累得無法接見他。最後，在李爾憤然地堅持之下，他們夫妻才肯出來見面。誰知，他竟然看到可恨的葛奈麗陪著一道出來！她跑來跟妹妹說自己的事，並慫恿妹妹反抗父王！

P. 112 這一幕讓李爾激動不已，尤其是看到麗晶還牽著葛奈麗的手。他問葛奈麗，看看他的灰白華鬢，難道她一點也不覺得慚愧嗎？麗晶則建議他和葛奈麗回去，並裁掉一半的隨從，求葛奈麗原諒他，兩人和平共處。她說畢竟他人老了，缺乏明辨事非的能力，得由心思縝密的人來帶他管他。

P. 113 要他屈膝下跪，乞求自己的女兒供他衣食？李爾覺得這實在是太荒謬了，他才不要這樣違背人倫地仰靠女兒。他說他決不會跟大女兒回去，他要和百名騎士留在麗晶這裡。他對麗晶說，怎麼說她都記得他把一半的國土送給了她，而且她的眼神溫和善良，不像葛奈麗那樣凶惡。他甚至說，要他跟葛奈麗回去，裁掉一半的侍從，那他寧可去法國，去跟娶小女兒而沒拿嫁妝的法王乞討一筆微薄的養老金呢。

　　看來李爾是大錯特錯了，麗晶待他的態度並不比姐姐好。她還好像故意要跟姐姐比不孝似地，說用五十名騎士來侍候他，她都嫌太多，二十五個就夠用了。

P. 114 李爾幾乎傷心斷腸，只得轉頭對葛奈麗說自己願意跟她回去，五十個還比二十五個多一倍，可見她的愛也是比麗晶多了一倍。

　　未料葛奈麗推諉說，為什麼需要二十五個這麼多的人來服侍呢？十個、五個都不需要啊，他大可使喚她的或妹妹的僕人呀！

　　這對沒有良心的姐妹好像在比賽，比看看誰對一向疼愛她們的老父親較狠心。她們想一點一滴地剝奪他所有的隨從，還有那曾經貴為國王的尊嚴呀！（對曾是一國之君的他來說，這點尊嚴少得可憐啊）

　　問題並不是擁有壯觀的隨從隊伍就會快樂，而是由國王變成乞求者，從統領百萬軍馬到半個隨從都沒有，豈談何容易啊！沒有隨從還是其次，負心女兒的拒絕更是傷透這可憐國王的心。

P.115 這些雙重的虐待和打擊，加上懊悔自己分配王國的昏庸，李爾開始有些神智不清。他無意識地咕咕噥噥，說誓言要報復這兩個沒有人性的妖婦，要讓她們嚐嚐慘絕人寰的報應！

P.117 就在他空口白話、滿口威脅時，黑夜驟然降臨，雷電交加，刮起轟聲隆隆的暴風雨。女兒們仍堅持不給他隨從，李爾於是要人把他的馬牽來，他寧願到外頭被狂風暴雨吹打，也不願和負心的女兒待在同一個屋簷下呀。女兒告訴他，如果一個人剛愎自用，讓自己受了傷，那也是理所當然的懲罰。說完她們就關上大門，任李爾在可怕的天候下離去。

老人家離開之際，狂風呼嘯，暴風雨愈來愈大。然而，女兒的不義遠比此時和大自然博鬥來得令人錐心。

P.118 李爾走了好幾哩路，一路上幾乎連半個灌木叢也沒有。他就在這樣狂風暴雨的黑夜荒原裡遊蕩，和狂風雷電相迎。他請求風把陸地捲進海裡，或是揚起海浪來淹沒大地，好讓像人類一樣忘恩負義的動物絕跡。

現在，惟一陪伴老國王的就只有卑微的愚者。愚者仍隨身在旁，盡力想用詼諧的話語來淡化不幸的遭遇。他說今晚是個搗蛋之夜，他們不過是出來泡泡水，國王最好還是回去，求女兒認同他：

只怪自己沒大腦，
嘿喲刮風又下雨！
可得安分來認命，
任他天天下雨天。

愚者還信誓旦旦說，美好今夜，正宜教女人不再傲慢。

P.120 曾是堂堂君王的李爾，在愚者冷冷清清陪伴著他時，永遠的好心忠僕肯特伯爵找到了他。肯特伯爵一直化身成凱爾斯緊隨著國王，但國王始終沒認出他。肯特說：「哎呦！大人，您在這裡啊？就算是夜行動物，也不會喜愛這樣的夜。可怕的暴風雨嚇得動物都躲回巢窩裡去了，人類的天性也是承受不了這種折磨和恐懼的呀。」

李爾回答，他有的是更大的痛苦，這種災難根本不算什麼。內心平靜時，才有閒工夫讓身體變得驕貴，而他內心裡的風暴，早讓他忘了所有的感官知覺，只剩激動的心跳。

他談到女兒的負心，說那簡直就像是嘴巴把拿東西餵它的手給咬下來。對兒女來說，父母就是他們的手、食物和一切呀。

P. 121 好心的凱爾斯仍一再懇求國王不要逗留屋外，最後終於說服他到荒原上一間破小的茅舍裡去避風雨。愚者先行進入茅舍，卻見他驚惶地往回跑，直呼自己看到了鬼。

P. 122 後來仔細一瞧，才發現那鬼不過是可憐的瘋乞丐，進來這空茅舍裡躲風避雨。瘋乞丐鬼話連篇，愚者聽了害怕。像他們這種可憐瘋子，不管是真瘋還是假瘋，反正是要迫使軟心腸的鄉下人給點施捨。他們在鄉間遊蕩，管自己叫做「可憐的湯姆」或「不幸的透力骨」，嘴裡嘟嚷著：「誰給可憐的湯姆賞點東西啊？」然後用別針、釘子或迷迭香的樹枝，把自己的手臂戳得流血。他們做這種嚇人的舉動，一邊祈禱，一邊瘋言瘋語地詛咒，起了憐憫心或被嚇到的無知鄉下人，就會給點施捨。

P. 123 眼前這可憐的傢伙就是這種瘋子。他全身赤裸，只在腰際圍了條毯子，國王見他處境如此淒慘，就想他必定也是一位把所有東西都給了女兒的父親，所以才落到了這樣的下場。除了女兒不孝，李爾想不出還有什麼原因可以讓人這麼悲慘。

聽到李爾說出這些奇怪的話，好心的凱爾斯看出來他的精神狀態顯然不穩定，女兒的虐待真把他給整瘋了。

現在，可敬的肯特伯爵又有了一個空前的好機會，可以在關鍵時刻表現忠誠。

P. 124 拂曉時分，在一些仍忠心耿耿的隨從的幫助下，肯特伯爵把國王護送到了多佛堡，因為伯爵的友人和人脈大都在那裡。隨後伯爵搭船前往法國，趕往蔻蒂莉的宮廷，如訴如泣地說明她父王的可憐處境，並對她姐姐的不仁不義指證歷歷。善良忠誠的蔻蒂莉聽得淚眼婆娑，她懇求夫君國王准許她搭船離開，帶一匹人馬回英格蘭征討狠心的女兒和女婿，好讓老父王復位。法王准予後，蔻蒂莉隨即出發，帶著皇家軍隊登陸多佛。

P. 125 好心的伯爵肯特派人照顧發瘋的李爾，結果李爾抓住了個機會，躲過侍從溜了出來。就在李爾在多佛近郊遊蕩時，恰巧被蔻蒂莉的隨從撞見。李爾當時真是狀極可悲呀，他完全瘋掉，一個人大聲唱歌，頭上戴著用稻草、蕁麻和麥田裡撿來的野草所編成的王冠。

蔻蒂莉急著想見父親，但大夫囑咐，最好在李爾睡過覺、服過他們開的草藥，讓精神鎮定了些後再相見比較好。

P. 126 蔻蒂莉承諾，要是這些醫術高明的大夫能夠讓老國王康復，她就把她所有的黃金珠寶都送給他們。不久，李爾的精神很快就康復到可以和女兒相認的狀況了。

父女團圓的光景，令人動容。這可憐的老國王百感交加，再見他曾深愛的孩子，他欣喜不已；再想到自己曾一怒之下為芝麻小事遺棄她，而她卻仍保一片孝心，他就又羞愧不已。歡喜與慚愧交雜，加上疾病的折騰，半瘋半癲的李爾有時忘了自己身在何處，搞不清楚輕吻他、親切地跟他講話的人是誰。

P. 127 之後他又會說，這位女子想來就是他的女兒蔻蒂莉吧，要是他搞錯了，也請大家不要見笑。李爾隨後跪了下來，乞求孩子原諒他。善良的蔻蒂莉也一直跪在他身邊，祈求上天保佑他。她表示他不應該下跪，她不過是盡應盡的孝道，她是他的孩子，是他如假包換的孩子蔻蒂莉！

她親吻父王，說要用她的吻撫平姐姐對他的傷害，又說她們該感到可恥，竟然把慈祥的白鬍老父趕到天寒地凍的屋外。蔻蒂莉傳神地形容，就算是敵人的狗咬了自己，在那樣的寒夜裡，也會讓那條狗偎在自己的爐火旁取暖的呀。

P. 129 她告訴父親，說她特地從法國來幫助他。而父親請她務必忘記過去並原諒他，表示自己又老又糊塗，根本不知道自己在做什麼。他告訴蔻蒂莉，她絕對有理由不愛他，可是她的姐姐沒有理由不孝。蔻蒂莉回答，她和姐姐一樣，沒有理由不愛他。

且讓這個孝順慈愛的孩子去守護老國王吧。其他兩位女兒為人狠心，這種可怕打擊逼得老國王精神錯亂，如今有了睡眠和治療，蔻蒂莉和大夫們終於讓他康復了。

P. 130 再說那兩個狠心的女兒吧。這兩個忘恩負義的惡人，對自己的老父親都這麼無情無義了，又怎麼可能對自己的丈夫忠實呢？她們很快就連裝裝守分恩愛的樣子都不耐煩了，還公開表示自己琵琶別抱。

好巧不巧的是，兩姐妹愛上了同一個人──艾德蒙。艾德蒙是前葛勞斯特伯爵的私生子，他叛變奪取原屬於合法繼承人艾德嘉兄弟的爵位，靠卑鄙的手段當上了伯爵。這個卑鄙的人和卑鄙的葛奈麗、麗晶，算是蛇鼠一窩了。

麗晶的丈夫康沃公爵死後，姐妹兩人出現爭端。待丈夫一死，麗晶就宣布要和葛勞賽斯特伯爵成親，使得姐姐不禁妒火中燒。原來，卑鄙的伯爵不只對麗晶示愛，也曾多次向葛奈麗表白。結果，葛奈麗竟找機會把妹妹給毒死。

P. 132 葛奈麗的丈夫歐伯尼公爵後來得知此事，又聽到她勾搭葛勞賽斯特伯爵的傳言，便把她打入牢裡。在愛情的挫折和憤恨之下，葛奈麗不久後就自盡。就這樣，天理公道終於作用在兩個缺德的女兒身上。

事情發生後一時嘩然，她們死有餘辜，人人莫不稱慶正義得到伸張。然後人們又轉移焦點，讚嘆公義的神奇力量，也同樣作用在善良小女兒蔻蒂莉的悲慘命運中。蔻蒂莉的善行理當得到更多的善報，然而，殘酷的真理是：在這個塵世上，純潔善良的人並不一定得到好報。

葛奈麗和麗晶派邪惡伯爵葛勞賽斯特所統領的軍隊，大獲勝利。手段卑鄙的伯爵，可不希望有人阻礙他篡奪王位，遂把蔻蒂莉害死獄中。

P.134 蔻蒂莉來人間示範感天的孝道後，上天就把這個純真的年輕女孩召喚到祂身邊了。她死後不久，李爾也隨即告別人世。

P.135 李爾從遭女兒虐待到悲傷謝世，好心的伯爵肯特始終守護著這位老主人。李爾在世時，肯特曾企圖讓他明白自己一直化名成凱爾斯跟隨著他，偏偏李爾已經因為抑鬱而神智不清，根本弄不清楚什麼跟什麼，搞不懂肯特和凱爾斯怎麼可能是同一個人。肯特便想，事到如今也毋需對他叨擾解釋。李爾不久撒手人寰，這位有了一把年紀的國王忠僕，在為老主人的悲苦而痛心之餘，很快也隨他共赴黃泉了。

天理最後又是如何作用在卑鄙伯爵葛勞賽斯特的身上呢？他謀反之事東窗事發，結果在和合法爵位繼承人的兄弟決鬥時一命嗚呼。至於葛奈麗的丈夫歐伯尼公爵，他與蔻蒂莉之死無關，也不曾慫恿妻子去做違逆父親的壞事，於是李爾死後他就登基為不列顛國王，但他的故事就不勞再敘。本篇故事要講的是李爾和三個女兒的故事，而如今他們都已經化為塵土了。